SOUTHERN STEEL

by

Sherrie H. Coombs

DORRANCE
PUBLISHING CO
EST. 1920
PITTSBURGH, PENNSYLVANIA 15238

Dorrance Publishing Co
585 Alpha Drive
Suite 103
Pittsburgh, PA 15238
Visit our website at *www.dorrancebookstore.com*

ISBN: 978-1-6480-4955-2
eISBN: 978-1-6480-4549-3

— CHAPTER 1 —

The sun was brilliant on that October day, so blinding that even the strongest protective sunglasses could not lessen its glare. As Sydney enjoyed the red, orange, and yellow maple leaves waving under the sunlight, she thought how this was her favorite time of year. The mornings were crisp, the afternoons warm, and the nights just chilly enough to roast marshmallows over an open fire pit. The perfect kind of weather to drive with the windows down, so the wind could whip through your hair.

But it was hard to relax and just drive while not thinking about the important meeting impending in a couple of hours, a meeting that would determine the future of her project that had consumed her days and nights for months. Many women loved shopping, nail salons and girls' nights out, but not Sydney James — not even close. Her life was filled with research, building prototypes, and corporate presentations. It was the intricate design work that made her life exciting, breathing fresh air in her lungs, and driving her career forward to create bigger, better, and more efficient products. The week had been tough with meetings that pushed Sydney to her limits. Her head ached from the intense focus her job required to be precise, perfect, and on-point. The long hours and fierce determination had won out in the end but had tested her to the point that others would have buckled beneath the pressure. It was almost over now. One more presentation via Skype and her week would end, hopefully on a high note, and she could relax, if only for a day or two before starting more research.

Speeding north on I-75 from Augusta, Sydney regretted her decision to stay in the business suit she wore for the early morning presentation. The white linen pants so neatly pressed at 7:00 this morning had wrinkled and felt snug around her thighs. Although the black silk camisole was cool against her skin, the linen jacket felt binding and uncomfortable scrunched under the restraints of the seatbelt. Her week had been packed with long meetings, contract negotiations and mind-blowing amounts of facts and figures but would be ending with the most important meeting for the financial quarter. If the meeting went as planned, Sydney James Engineering would sign a major contract that would be her reward for months of hard work and allow her to spend the next six to nine months developing and researching, which was the best part of her career... Well, research and the staggering contract pay-outs.

As the radio played an old country ballad, Syd's prestigious BMW 750 was hugging the highway when she felt it. Her car, one of the rare loves of her life, had missed a stroke. It was just a tiny skip and ever so slight, but she felt it. Her baby with its Turbo 322 performance engine, which was a perfect, well-oiled, finely tuned driving machine skipped a beat. It was almost not there at all, but for Sydney's highly trained senses, cat-like eyes, and razor-sharp ears, there was a miss. To some, this would mean little if anything at all. Even a slight skip or two in an engine so pristine might indicate the need for an oil change in the near future. It might even mean the warning to schedule an early tune up soon. But Sydney James was a professional engine designer. She was a Harvard graduate, a master designer from MIT, and had worked with teams from around the world creating superior performance engines. This German engine was not one of Sydney's designs, but it was the powerhouse for her car that she wore like a glove. This sweet ride was her mobile office much of the time and even became her home away from home when she was traveling, like today. She knew every square inch of the engine, every stitch in its creamy leather interior, and every thread in the plush mats where she only drove in bare feet. She could diagram every part under her hood in the middle of her sleep at night. If there was a skip in the engine, she would know it...and she knew it. This could not happen now, no time was a good time, but certainly not when she was 75 miles south of her next meeting without a second to spare. Friday afternoon traffic was sure to be a nightmare, and soon, she would hit the weekend jam just north of Atlanta driving through Marietta and rushing to arrive in Chattanooga by 6:00.

Skip—she felt it again. It was there, or was it?

"Dang it, I know I felt it." She knew this engine and treated it like a spoiled only-child. On any other day, she would pull over and check under the hood to see what the problem could be and then be on her way, but today of all days, she did not have the luxury of time.

Sydney decided to drive on. Her BMW was a car of precision and endurance, not just beauty. Oh, she was a beauty alright, with her sleek white mother of pearl double coated paint and high gloss finish, ultra-soft cream-colored interior, and every bling and option offered by BMW. Sydney named her Beautiful Betty when her custom ordered car was delivered last year, and she still felt an intense sense of pride every time she slid into her driver's seat and listened as the silky-smooth engine came to life. Surely Betty would perform well for her today. This little beauty wouldn't let her down on this important day.

Seventy-five miles was just a skip in the park for this perfect piece of machinery, and no harm would come if she drove north for another hour or so. But then there it was again; she felt another skip then a hesitation and knew she could not ignore it this time.

— CHAPTER 2 —

Matthew Daniels, CEO of Daniels Engineering, waited for no one. He was a man of a sharp mind, sharper dress, and even sharper tongue. But this meeting would have to wait; the presentation would have to be put on hold. He just didn't know it yet. The engineering firm that Matthew built and ran flawlessly took a back seat to nothing. He was a driving force and few crossed him, certainly no one asked him to wait for them. However, beneath his tough exterior, Matt was a great guy, and he knew Sydney very well. The two had met in college and became close friends. Even after they graduated, went their separate ways, and formed their own companies, they continued to work together on various projects throughout the years. They had a mutual respect for the work each produced and were a perfect professional pair. Their work ethic, stamina, and demand for perfection were second to none. The scheduled meeting with Sydney was just a formality for him and his team. He wanted the engine; he knew that Syd designed it, and there was no question that it was exceptional. The money was allocated for the purchase of the patent, and all that was left was to sign on the dotted line. The deal was hers, and they both knew it. But for Sydney, the process could never be that simple. She drove herself at a ferocious pace, never letting up, never shutting down, and never once in her career requested a delay on a prototype presentation, even with Matt. It was beyond all that she was taught by her father, by her education, and by her own high standards to offer subpar performance for any reason. However, if anyone would understand that she needed to wait until Monday, Matt would be the one. He treated his own automobiles like the sleek machines they were created to be. If one of his cars missed a stroke during a drive, he would surely stop to investigate the issue. Matt would understand completely, wouldn't he? Sydney pulled into a parking lot where she dialed Matthew's cell number to explain her situation.

"Hello, Matthew Daniels speaking," he brusquely answered.

"Hi Matt, it's Sydney. I have a situation and need to ask your team to postpone our presentation until Monday."

"Of course, Syd, what's up? Anything I can do to help you? It must be serious for you to cancel a meeting. I don't think...nope, I know... I've never known you to cancel anything in your life. You can't even cancel a magazine subscription. Is there a problem with the prototype? Oh, God, don't tell me you have to stop production." Matt was not a patient man.

"No, no, not at all. It's my personal car. I am on 75 North coming into Marietta, and my engine has started skipping. Just a couple of misses at first, and I let it slide. But now I have felt it a few more times. No check engine lights or indicators are on, but you know me; I can't let anything happen to my Beautiful Betty. I need to stop by the parts store and pick up a plug or filter or at least see if I can run a diagnostic check. With this Friday traffic, I know I will be late for our meeting. I'd rather wait until Monday when my mind is fresh rather than rush in and be unprepared."

"Don't give it a second thought, Syd. Go take care of your baby. Get her purring again, and let's meet Monday at 2:00."

With a sigh of relief, Sydney thanked Matthew and ended the call. It wasn't until she buckled her seat belt that she realized she was sweating heavily in her linen suit and not because she was hot, but because she was completely stressed due to calling out on a meeting; a first for Sydney James.

— CHAPTER 3 —

Searching *Google* on her phone, Sydney found the nearest
Extreme Auto store to be 12 miles north, and away she drove.
Extreme Auto was a national chain of supply stores that stocked
only the best quality parts for the persnickety car owners,
specialty mechanics, and even race car teams. The prices were
not cheap, but when performance was the objective, there was
no cutting corners. Pulling into the lot, Sydney chose the space
nearest to the front door in case she needed to use an outlet for
air tools. After raising the hood and examining the engine, she
knew exactly the parts she would replace. Once home and in her
personal garage, Betty's engine would get a complete detailing,
but today, this would be fine. Leaving the hood open, Sydney
walked into the store and stood at the counter for what seemed
like an hour. Her patience was wearing thin with the slow
service, and she knew the first changes she would make if she
owned this franchise would be to hire a capable front desk clerk.
Two, three, five minutes later a giant of a man slumbered to the
front in no hurry at all. He was wearing dirty jeans and a blue
mechanic's shirt sporting a name tag which proudly displayed
"Doug" on the patch.

"Can I help you, little lady?" Doug asked as he cleaned a carburetor in his massive greasy hands.

Oh God almighty, just what she needed, a hero trying to rescue her.

"Yes, I need an air filter please. I need the Mann C3698/3-2, and I may need a Bosch OE Specialty Nickel spark plug for a 2018 BMW 750i," Sydney replied abruptly because she felt sticky and irritable in her current situation.

"You sure that what's you need, hon?" asked Doug in a slow country drawl.

"Uh yes, hon," responded Sydney in her sarcastic northern accent.

"Well, sweetie, I don't know if we have that model, we might have ta order it for ya. With it being a Friday afternoon and all, ya might have to wait 'till Monday. Will that be alright with yer husband?" crooned Doug in his most superior voice.

"No, it will not be fine, and I don't need to ask my husband. It is for my vehicle, and I need it now. It is imperative that I purchase one this afternoon, so that I can repair my car and be on my way. If you do not have it, will you find it for me at another store in the near vicinity?" Sydney was losing patience quickly with this mountain of a grease monkey and his patronizing attitude.

"Let me just check my computer here and see if we have one in stock." Doug looked at Sydney for her approval.

"If you are waiting for me to say go, then please accept my permission, uh Doug." Sydney stood tapping her foot unconsciously while reading his name tag.

"This computer ain't gonna work any faster by you tap dancin' with those pretty lil' feet," Doug said as he looked at her over his computer screen.

It was evident that he was toying with her, but she was not amused. When Doug stared back at Sydney, she noticed he had sky blue eyes and a thick screen of lashes that were wasted on a man. He began babbling about air filters and spark plugs, which did not impress Sydney in the least. She knew what she needed to purchase and tried to block out his mumbling.

"Well looky here, I believe we have what yer lookin' for swee... uh ma'am," drawled Doug. As he went down the aisle to find the supplies Sydney needed, she noticed his greasy hands and pants that looked like they had never seen soap or a washing machine. He handed her the boxes and took her credit card for payment.

"Why are you so dirty?" Sidney asked Doug after she paid for her items. "Now there is grease on the box of this product and my card, and it seems to me that a front desk attendant should appear clean and professional. I will never understand why men cannot work on engines and remain clean. Does your boss know you greet customers dressed like this?" Sydney knew she was being bitchy, but she really didn't care at the moment. Her nerves were completely frazzled.

"Well, I'm not the front desk attendant ma'am. I am the manager of the store, and it just so happens that my desk clerk didn't show up today. I have been answering phones, helping customers, and trying to repair an engine that seems to have bit the bullet," Doug said as he scratched his head. The grease under his nails made it evident that he had been under a hood attempting to wrestle an unyielding beast.

Syd paid for the parts and said, "Thank you for your assistance," as she strolled out of the store. Her exit did not go unnoticed. Doug watched as Sydney opened her trunk and brought out a black quilted mat which she spread over the fender of her BMW to prevent scratching the car paint or staining her clothes. As she bent over the car her white linen pants clung to her hips and Doug noticed how fine she looked in her outfit. Her pants stretched into a perfect heart across her bottom, and even though she was wearing a jacket, he could only imagine how she would look spread across that hood wearing less than her current pants and top. Even though she was obviously someone's spoiled trophy wife, he decided she just might need his assistance again.

"Need some help under there?" asked Doug taking a closer look at her tight white pants.

"No, thank you sir," Sydney replied oblivious to his delight in her position across the car. "I can manage; I sort of know what I am doing."

"That so?" Doug replied, even though he doubted that she had ever seen underneath a hood. He imagined her days filled with manicures, pedicures, and spending her husband's credit cards.

"Really it is so. I'm quite able to change my own air filter and spark plug. However, if I find that I need a handyman, I will certainly let you know." Sydney knew she was being a smart ass, but she didn't care. She was tired, hungry, and wanted to be on the road headed north. She hated being patronized by men and had dealt with their condescending attitudes her entire adult life. In a matter of minutes, Sydney had replaced the parts, returned her tools to her spotlessly organized trunk, and cleaned the repair area and surface of her beloved Betty. When she started the engine, the car hummed like a song bird, and Sydney hoped the problem was solved. She closed the hood and was ready to be on her way. Doug was very impressed with her knowledge of the car engine as well as her ability to work fast and look cute at the same time. She was tiny and pristine in her white suit, which was stain free even after working with engine grease. How did she do that?

"May I please wash up in your restroom?" Syd asked with a scowl on her face.

"You bet, come on inside," offered Doug.

After Sydney scrubbed up to her elbows she emerged and saw Doug in the back garage stall with his head buried underneath the hood and staring at the engine he was working on. She had heard him curse a couple of times while she was washing up, and he didn't notice her coming into the bay.

Sydney wanted to thank him for his offer of assistance ,and she didn't want him to think of her as a complete jerk.

"Thanks for your assistance; I'm sorry if I came off as a grump. It's been a rough day, and I'm ready to be home. Looks like you're having engine troubles of your own," Sydney observed, drying her hands. She couldn't resist an engine in distress. She had removed the white linen jacket before changing the parts on her B-mer and was wearing a loose-fitting black silk tank top that revealed smooth, firm arms and satin shoulders. Doug was not blind.

"Yes, dammit. She won't budge. I have tried everything I know; I think I've changed every part and still can't get her running. Not a problem I have very often with women," he smirked.

"I'm sure," Sydney replied in complete sarcasm. "Mind if I take a look?" she suggested more than asked.

"Be my guest, but don't say I didn't warn you. She's a little witch," Doug said as he wiped the sweat across his forehead.

Sydney looked under the hood as the engine glared back at her. She instructed Doug to adjust the GC sprocket. Then she handed him a timing light and told him to adjust the fiber guides on both of the timing chains. After a few minor adjustments, she watched the as timing self-corrected. Sydney walked around to driver's seat and fired up the engine. It came to life and purred like a kitten.

"What the? ...I can't believe this. I have been working on this engine for two days straight with no results and some broke down little Housewife of Atlanta walks in and fixes the problem. I'll be damned," huffed Doug. Even though he was embarrassed at her success, a crooked smile was on his face, and he obviously appreciated her talents with an engine. He stood scratching his head as Sydney walked out of the bay.

"You're welcome," Sydney sneered over her shoulder, not realizing Doug was right behind her. After walking to her car, she turned around and handed Doug a business card and told him to give her a call if he ever needed a *real* mechanic. She started her car, fastened her seatbelt, and drove north toward home, exhausted but pleased that her baby was running smoothly, without a miss.

— CHAPTER 4 —

SCJ International Steel, LLC
Sydney C James, PE, CEO
Chief Engine Designer and Mechanical Engineer

Doug planned a trip around the first of November each year to visit his family. Holidays were always so chaotic with his emotional his sister and her young daughters, so for years Doug had visited them in early November to satisfy his required appearance for Thanksgiving and Christmas. He loved his family but could only handle them in small doses. Doug's mother was very doting and his father slept most of the holidays in his recliner watching football. Sister Becca knew all the latest gossip that she felt the need to share, but Doug was never interested. Her tiny tots had bouncing blond curls and ran around squealing, trying to scare the cat. Theirs was a typical family, but Doug led a quiet life, and he liked his solitude. The small community where he lived as a child offered little for him to develop a business, so early on Doug decided to move to a larger city near Atlanta where there were more opportunities for a lead specialty mechanic. Doug had considered becoming a diesel mechanic and once applied to work for Delta Airlines but was never called for an interview, probably due to his lack of education and experience. Actually, Doug knew that his heart and talent hid beneath car engines ranging from small economy cars to Italian race cars that could easily hit 200 miles per hour. He had the need for speed, and there was nothing that could compare to the sweet sound of a velvety smooth engine. Beneath a hood is where Doug found fire for his soul. During his high school years, football had been an outlet, and Doug excelled as a defensive tackle. He accepted a scholarship to the University of Georgia but couldn't cut academics and athletics, so he dropped football after his first season. He stayed in school until his final year, and when his father was diagnosed with cancer, he moved back home to help his family with finances. After Doug walked in one night and found his girlfriend Jennifer dancing under the sheets with his best friend Steve, he lost all interest in college and dating. He buried his head under every automobile hood that needed attention and discovered his new passion in the arms of a well-oiled engine. In his hometown, gossip ran high but incomes ran low, so once Doug decided to move in the direction of Atlanta, he never looked back. He needed time to mend a broken heart and build a career.

As Doug drove north, he thought how his hometown was only half an hour away from Chattanooga. Chattanooga, Tennessee, a town that loved SEC football, summer festivals by the river, and was the hometown to Sydney James. Sydney was a woman who knew too much about car engines, a woman that rejected his flirtations, a woman that looked so sexy on a warm October Friday four weeks prior, and a woman he could not get out of his mind. Doug's thoughts wandered to Sydney's confidence in her knowledge of engines. He had never met a woman who knew her way around a car except in the backseat. She wasn't like the few girls he knew in high school ,who were willing to hand him a wrench or screwdriver while listening to his car sound system. She was in command; Sydney seemed to know her way around a car like most women knew a shopping mall. But she had not been very nice at all; perhaps she had a steel heart...southern steel. He had tried to lighten her mood on the day they met, but she was having none of it. Obviously, she had a mission, and banter wasn't a part of it. Why did he even give her a second thought? It wasn't like she was all that; hell, she wasn't even grateful when he helped her replace her filter and spark plug. To be honest, Doug hadn't assisted her at all. He stood back and watched as she replaced the parts quickly and efficiently, seemingly without any effort. She didn't talk but worked without distraction and was totally oblivious to how she was taunting him in her tight pants and thin, silky top.

Late one night before bed, Doug *Googled* her name to find that Sydney Cherrill James had grown up near the midsized town of Chattanooga, and she was smart, extremely smart...a southern girl without a southern girl charm. She attended a private middle and high school then moved north to enroll at the University of Tennessee in Knoxville. Her perfect 1600 on the SAT exam landed her several scholarship offers in math and engineering, and one was from Harvard. After two years at UT, Sydney decided to head north and transferred to the Ivy League to complete her degree as a double major in biochemistry and business management. Once Sydney earned her undergraduate degree from Harvard, she entered the engineering world at MIT with a concentration in automotive engine design. At 24, Sydney graduated top of her class with a master's degree in mechanical design and performance specialization. Her PhD thesis won awards for research in engine precision and development. And it was published into an instruction book that only a rocket scientist could appreciate. Obviously, she knew her way around an engine, and Doug realized he had met a mechanical genius. Nothing in her bio reported a husband or children and not even one episode on *The Real Housewives of Atlanta*.

The number on her business card went straight to voice mail, and Doug left a message seriously doubting he would ever hear from her. She probably didn't even remember him even though he knew she would remember the day her car had trouble. She told him to give her a call if he was ever in the area, and this week, he was in the area. She had invited him to Chattanooga to see what a "real mechanic" could do, so maybe he would take her up on her offer. Perhaps he would see just what her business was all about. She most likely ran some stuffy company which specialized in selling car parts from Japan. After all, her card did read International. Sydney would only remember him as the dumb mechanic who couldn't even bring his own engine to life. She had not been impressed with his mechanical knowledge and certainly not his attempts at conversation. She appeared aloof and irritable. He wondered why he was even curious about her. Doug was surprised when his cell rang a few hours later, and it was Sydney returning his call.

"Hello Doug, what a coincidence that you left me a message, I've been thinking about you. I'm glad you called," said Sydney in a professional manner.

"Really? I mean, really, me to, "Doug stammered.

"Yes, I have something I'd like to discuss with you. I was actually going to give you a call next week and ask if you could come to Chattanooga to meet with me," Sydney told him.

"Well, actually, I am in the area this weekend. I usually come to visit my parents for a pre-holiday visit, and so here I am. How about tomorrow or Sunday before I head back to Atlanta?" Doug asked.

"Absolutely. Could you spare a couple of hours to visit my garage?" Sydney inquired.

"Your garage? Sure, your car giving you trouble? Do you need my expert advice again?" Doug snickered, but Sydney ignored his joke.

"Hardly. Could we meet tomorrow at 2:00? My address is on my business card," she informed Doug, and he was certainly intrigued. What on Earth could she want to show him?

"I have it and can be there tomorrow at 2:00. I'll find your place," Doug replied.

Sydney said goodbye and hung up the phone. She remembered his bright blue eyes and then her second thought of him was an impression she wanted to forget; a greasy mechanic's shirt. She also remembered his appearance and hoped he had clean clothes to wear. However, there were a couple of points that could work in her favor if she proceeded with her plan. First of all, Sydney liked the fact that Doug was not threatened by her knowledge of engines. He listened and took her suggestions with ease and followed her lead, which helped bring his engine back to life. Although he flirted with her, she felt like it was harmless banter, and he seemed to be capable of focusing for longer than two-point-five seconds. Sydney needed to hire a good mechanic, and she believed that Doug could become one. He obviously had some business knowledge, or he would not have become the manager of a national chain auto parts store. She had been searching for an assistant who would not run off with the first little hottie that shook her tail feathers at him. Sydney had been down that road before and had no desire to repeat it. Her company was very different than the type of work he performed now. Could he handle the pressure of the deadlines? Not meeting specifications could result in millions of dollars in fines. Would he even be interested in listening to her idea? Perhaps he liked his job enough that he would have no desire to change his career.

Well, she wouldn't know until she asked him, and after they talked, she may decide that this position was not right for either of them. Syd certainly had mixed feelings about seeing him again and hoped he had a clean outfit to wear.

— CHAPTER 5 —

Two o'clock sharp the next day, her doorbell rang, and Sydney went down the stairs to open the door for Doug. There he stood in decent jeans and a button down shirt—grease free—with those eyes.

"Hello Doug, please come in." Sydney shook his hand and looked like a young girl in her jeans and sneakers. "Welcome to my home, come on upstairs."

Sydney opened the door for him to come into her foyer. As he looked Sydney over, he remembered her stuffy attitude when they first met, but she seemed much more relaxed here in her own environment. He hoped her reception of him was more relaxed as well.

Her home was an old renovated warehouse, and he admired his surroundings. The massive wooden door was from the early 1900s and had been sanded and finished in a deep stain that revealed old dents and scratches hiding time trusted secrets. The old building had been a paper business that opened in 1927 and closed in 1953. For years, the brick walls chipped away, and when Sydney purchased it five years earlier, she knew she wanted to keep the industrial integrity beneath its rafters to match the engine design business she planned to open.

As Doug stepped inside the large foyer, he noticed the exposed brick walls extended all the way to the high ceilings where black industrial ducts hung suspended by silver metal straps. Sydney took Doug's jacket and hung it on a large hook mounted on the brick wall that had been made from an old horse saddle. The entrance wall in front of him was old whitewashed wood and was decorated with a distressed sofa table that looked like it belonged in an old farmhouse. A tall bouquet of fresh cut flowers in a crystal vase stood over six feet against the wall. The large water color painting in pale pinks, blues, and neutrals that hung on the wall to the right of the flowers looked as if an artist had splashed grainy paint across the canvas just to make it look and feel like a beach scene. Sailboats and wispy clouds invited the viewer into its cool blue waters, creating the sense of gliding across the smooth ocean and being lulled to sleep. The area was very simple with minimal furnishings and created a warm homey feel.

"Awe, you shouldn't have bought flowers for the occasion, but I appreciate the effort," Doug teased.

"I actually keep fresh flowers all over my loft," Syd explained. "After working around men and grease all week, I appreciate a feminine touch." No matter why she bought them, Doug thought the touch was beautiful and classic, like Sydney.

The room immediately welcomed him and brought a sense of peace. Sydney led the way up the old, wide staircase made of original hardwood that had seen better years but shone like a new penny underneath layers of a rich polyurethane finish. Syd had spent hours sanding each step to reach the perfect shine she wanted. Thick wrought iron railings secured the heavy staircase to the wall and landing above. The same floors were in her living space, and if she wore thick socks, she could slide from one end of her loft to her bedroom at the other end. This was her sanctuary, and her personality was deeply imprinted into every inch of her personal space.

"Thank you for coming, I hope you find me nicer than our original meeting. I apologize for my gruff reception; I was having an extremely stressful day."

As Sydney led the way Doug admired her tight jeans and pale blue, sleeveless shirt. She was not wearing flirty clothes, but something about her body spelled sexy, and his mind began to wander.

"No problem, I'm glad you stopped by my store that day. You ended up being my knight in shining armor coming to my rescue with the timing issue. I had been looking in a completely different direction when the obvious was right in front of me. I admit I am curious about what you have to show me or why you would even need my advice."

Doug looked around her home and noticed the exotic pieces of art and thought how high maintenance she must be. The airy second floor was open and obviously designed for Sydney to spend a good amount of her time here. A sprawling white leather sectional couch in the middle of the room was covered with pillows of all shapes and sizes. There were small pillows in creamy neutrals made of wool and thick fabrics, medium and large knotty cotton pillows in designs of zigzag and geometric patterns. The couch looked like whipped cream and would be a great place to sink into after a hard day's work. Doug had no idea how many nights Sydney fell asleep on the couch as she snuggled with a good book and glass of wine. Two sturdy, dark gray chairs flanked each side of the couch with coordinating pillows and a gray and ivory rug covered almost the entire sitting space. Behind the seating area sat a farmhouse table and eight mismatched chairs that somehow worked as a suite. There was an exposed brick fireplace that Sydney whitewashed and displayed an enormous oak mantle stained in a rich dark finish. A 72 inch HD TV hung above a gas fireplace which indicated that Sydney did not chop wood during a cold winter...nope, no chopping wood for those soft hands. The large kitchen was open to the living space and was well equipped with sleek modern stainless appliances. Gray and black granite countertops coordinated with a herringbone tile backsplash and white shaker style cabinets decorated with flat black handles. A large white apron farmhouse sink, double ovens and commercial size refrigerator made Doug smile at the thought of Sydney preparing a home cooked meal for the holidays. This girl must want her guests to think she was a chef. Everything in her home was in coordinating colors of soft whites and various shades of gray and had neither a feminine nor masculine touch. The colors were all neutrals; very relaxing and welcoming.

"I really like what you've done with this old warehouse," commented Doug as he looked around appreciating her taste in decoration.

"Thanks, I love it here," Sydney agreed as she glanced around her loft. "It's my solace from the crazy circles I run in my daily life. It's peaceful and quiet, and I can shut out the world. I have pieces here from my entire life, and it helps me to feel close to my dad." Sydney pointed out three large clay pieces on her shelves that she had purchased in Turkey, one from Haiti, and a few wooden sculptures from a trip to China. Doug noticed a nostalgic look in her eyes as she ran her hands over the pieces and he could easily recognize sadness from the loss of her parents.

"May I take a look around?" Doug asked.

"Oh certainly, make yourself at home. Can I get you a drink, soda, beer, bourbon?" Syd asked as she headed to the kitchen for beverages.

"A beer would be great," Doug replied as he strolled into her bedroom appreciating its more feminine touch.

The ceilings stood at least 30 feet tall and as he looked around he spotted her bedroom beyond the kitchen. Her king-sized bed was tall with a high shiplap headboard but dwarfed under the tall ceilings. The iron rail canopy held white flowing sheers around each corner that wisped lightly each time the central air came on. The white down covers were thick and the bed was topped pillows of soft cottons, silks and nylons that made it appear cloud-like. Her bedroom furnishings looked vintage and could have been from a previous era, maybe even her parents. Each piece was painted in white and distressed to look old and worn. There was a photo of a little girl, a puppy, and a man on her dresser, and Doug decided this must be her father. He picked up the photograph and saw the little freckle-face girl who must have been Sydney looking up adoringly at her father. She was obviously a daddy's girl. There were two guitars mounted on the wall across from her bed, and as Doug was somewhat of a music buff, he knew one was a Gibson and the other a Fender, each in good condition. They looked like maybe from the early 50s and were probably worth a mint.

"Do you play the guitar?" Doug was curious about her hidden talents.

"No, those were my dad's. He loved country music and played locally with his friends. I play piano, but I never took guitar lessons," Sydney explained.

The tall windows were framed by billowy sheers and waved in unison with the canopy sheers. Fresh flowers in tall shattered glass vases and white wide base candles decorated the tops of her chest and dresser. This room was simple, elegant, and very Sydney. Doug was learning that she was a woman of simplicity; elegant and simple. The master bath made his mind stray to areas it should not, but the deep soaking tub and glass shower caused him to imagine that several adults could easily fit. The whitewashed walls had no windows, but white subway tiles sparkled beneath nostalgic farm lights mounted on the wall. No makeup trays, no hairbrushes, no lace, no frills...just elegant and simple...but my, how sexy.

"This place is great," Doug stated as he took the cold beer from Sydney and thanked her. "No pets? No kids? No roommate?"

"No time," Syd replied. "It takes time and investment to keep a pet, or a kid. I have neither. If you will notice I have no living plants either, case closed. I replace the fresh flowers once a week, and that is the extent of my nurturing ability." Actually, Sydney would have loved to have a dog, but she just didn't have the time because she traveled so much with her job. Her entire childhood, she had dogs; she adored them, but for now, no time.

"We always had dogs when I was a little girl. My dad was known around our community for taking in stray dogs and treating whatever ailments they limped in with, and somehow, they never left our farm. He also grew a vast garden each summer and passed out extra produce to our neighbors. But he came home each night from work, I do not. He had time to invest in animals and other projects, and again, I just don't have that luxury."

As an only child, the mutts around her home became Sydney's best friends. Her memory took her back to Snowball, Sargent, Penny, Black Jack, and many others who stole her heart over the years. Shaking her head, she filed the sweet memories away and came back to the present.

"Absolutely, no time," she replied.

— CHAPTER 6 —

"Well Doug, I didn't ask you here to give you a grand tour of my apartment and reminiscence about my childhood. There is actually a method to my madness, and if we can go into my office, I'd like to discuss an idea I have thinking about."

They walked down a short hallway, and Sydney led Doug into an office befitting any corporate executive from a Fortune 500 company. Against the far wall, a large metal desk and a ragged leather office chair were surrounded by four computers that lined the workspace. On the brick walls behind the desk hung awards by Red Dot recognizing her for the G2150-200hp engine, one award from UKi Media & Events Automotive Magazine for the International Engine Design of the Year, Team Engine Graduate Leadership Award, and AIAA Foundation Engine Design Awards as well as several others that looked equally impressive. There were at least 20 awards ranging from 2005 to 2017, and all looked very important. Some of the awards were presented to Sydney James, some SCJ International Enterprises, and others Sydney James Professional Engineer. Doug was impressed. She was talented, smart, beautiful, and very successful.

Sydney saw Doug looking at her old desk and office furniture.

"Don't be jealous of my fine furnishings," she smiled. "These were all in my dad's office at his dealership. I would spin around and around in this chair as a child and play at this old metal desk, pretending I was his boss. I played with his calculator, running paper receipts onto the floor, and he never once fussed at me for making a mess. That old beat up filing cabinet was his and still holds his past customers' information that he filed away years before computers were used in the corporate world. I still use his old Rolodex with important phone numbers on it. There's not enough money to buy one piece of this furniture from me. I see the desk, and I see my dad."

"You have saved everything he left behind, haven't you?" Doug observed.

"He was my world, as a child and young woman. I just wish he would have lived to see what I am doing now," Syd said. "He taught me about engines, farm tractors, and lawn mowers, weed eating machines, boats, Chevys, imports, and his favorite, Fords. There wasn't an engine he wouldn't try to repair and most of the time he worked out the problems. I spent my childhood underneath the hood of a car or in the middle of some greasy gasoline or diesel engine. I loved it, and it shaped me into who I am today." Sydney's throat tightened from emotion when she tried to continue talking.

"Where was your mother during all of those years?" asked Doug when he noticed she had not mentioned her. He thought perhaps she had died earlier in Sydney's life.

"My mom left when I was 10 years old. My father was a heavy drinker and abusive to her when he drank too much. He was never mean to me, but she could say nothing right, and he hit her many times during his drunken episodes putting her in the hospital with broken bones and busted lips. It took me years in therapy to understand that she left for survival. I was his only baby, and she always said we were joined at the hip. Mom knew he would never let me go with her, so she left. She was in and out of my life during my teenage years, but my dad was my constant." Sydney looked sad as she talked about her childhood. "I don't talk about my past often, and if you ever open my Pandora's Box to anyone, I will never tell you anything else, no second chances. As a matter of fact, everything that goes on in my life and business is confidential, understood?" She had a determined look of steel in her eyes.

"Who are you really, Sydney James?" asked Doug with a side grin and blue eyes that glistened. "You work in a man's world, and obviously, you are very successful at it. You are extremely private and love your solitude yet travel frequently around the globe. You seem to be a happy person, but you have a sad past. Who's in there?" Doug tapped Sydney's head with his finger wondering how that amazing brain really worked in this little sprite of a woman.

Sydney tipped her chin upwards as she answered, "I am the daughter of a Ford engineer. He taught me to love cars, boats, motorcycles, and anything that runs. I learned to drive a tractor on a farm, I studied hard, worked harder than any man in my classes, and now I am the brains behind Sydney Cherrill James Engineering Design. I research, create, strategize, tweak, and perfect engine prototypes for companies all over the world. I am the go-to company for all things that run by gasoline, diesel, or a mixture. I live, eat, and breathe engines. I have contracts with some of the smallest and largest companies in many countries, and in my heart, I feel that I am an engine. I believe my blood is actually motor oil. We are one in the same, our hearts beat as one, and it's as if I commune with each engine and can actually feel its pulse and spirit. That is why I could help with your engine the day I stopped by your store. I could hear its defect, I could feel the vibration of the miss, sort of like a blind person feeling his way by searching for a beat."

Doug stared at her, finding her fascinating.

"That's where you come in. When I met you last month, I was having a horrible day. My car began to skip a beat every few miles. I sensed it as much as felt it. I felt the sluggish lack of pull for a few miles when I tried to pass a car before there was actually a skip. I had just finished a very important meeting in Augusta and was coming home to an equally important meeting here in Chattanooga. I needed to repair my car, not overhaul it, and just bandage it enough to get home safely and Skype into my webinar. That did not happen. I had to call my potential sponsor and postpone the meeting for the following Monday, a first in my entire career. I was sweaty, hungry and frustrated, made obvious by my behavior and attitude. Even though we had a rocky beginning, your country banter and attempts at flirting humored me; you patronized me as a woman and didn't take me seriously as a female mechanic. But when I walked into your bay, which was your own personal work space, you respected my knowledge just by watching me work on my BMW. You immediately responded to my suggestions on your engine without question. You took my lead, followed my instructions, and your engine sang a new song. You didn't appear threatened, and you even thanked me for my input. Those actions alone spoke volumes about you as a mechanic and a man. Would you like to do that again?" Sydney asked him almost timidly.

"Do what again? Work on that engine? It's running fine now. She doesn't have a hitch, thanks to you. I don't need to do that again." Doug looked puzzled.

"Not with that particular engine, but with another, and then another, and even more after that. I am considering offering you a position with my company, Doug. You follow directions, you know engines, maybe not like I do, but in a different way. My engine knowledge is in my brain, and yours is in your hands. I know how to design engines, but I can't put the man power and brute strength into them. I don't run my company alone even though I am a loner.

I need help. Any great leader knows it takes more than one person to succeed. My company structure is small at the top tier but branches out into larger divisions, much like a pyramid. I am the top level with one lead Mechanical Production Manager, and that would be you. I do not answer to a Board of Directors, I only answer to the sponsors that contribute funding for any particular project. After I design a prototype, the blueprint is sent to the architect for approval; once approved, the designs are then sent to a manufacturer where they are made and returned for additional tweaking and assembling until it comes to life. The majority of the times I have been commissioned to design a particular engine based on the client's needs, but if not, I will market my ideas to companies across the world. That is where the travel comes in, and there would be extensive travel for you as well. It is an intense position, and we would work side by side. This is not an ordinary nine-to-five type of job. I put in 60, sometimes 80-hour weeks and expect the same from my assistant. The liability is staggering in engine design as we are taking people's lives in our hands and responsible to keep them safe. There is very little time for an outside life, and I expect complete dedication to the company. You would be required to sign a confidentiality contract as well as a noncompeting agreement.

"This is my life, Doug, and I am not willing to compromise in any way. If we feel this might be a good fit, I will offer you an opportunity beyond any you could ever receive at your current company. You can read a manual and follow the instructions, right?"

Doug stared at her yet almost smiled at her and demeaning question.

"This is a serious question, and I am not making light of it because the majority of mechanics cannot read intrinsic instructions of manuals; they just go by instinct and raw talent, which is fine. However, in this position it is imperative to be able to apply every single word and follow step by step instructions, not skipping one single step, no questions asked. Do you believe you can do that?" Sydney asked.

"Yes, I can. I can follow any instruction manual, but I'm no match for these," said Doug as he pointed to the many awards on the wall. "This is way out of my league."

"Those are engineering awards, and I don't need another engineer, I hold that degree. I need a mechanic and a damn good one. Are you a good mechanic, Doug? Even perhaps a great one?" Syd asked.

"Yes, I am." Doug replied confidently.

"Would you consider becoming a great mechanic and production manager? It's a full-time job; you will have to move to Chattanooga, and as I mentioned, we will work together every day. I work hard and push harder. I am a perfectionist, and I can be tough. I work in a man's world, and I have to fight for the respect I receive. We will fight, and we will disagree, but I make all final decisions, no questions asked. I am the brain behind the brawn. You will curse me, and you will hate me, but if you will stick with me, you will become a part of something much bigger than yourself, bigger than the both of us, and you will contribute in ways you have never thought possible. My designs go way beyond engines in vehicles. You will be very surprised by the types of corporations that hire me to design prototypes for them. You will be required to travel to countries you may have only read about, and the confidentiality contract will cost you five million dollars if you break it. You will make more money than you could possibly make at Auto Extreme, even as a National Manager. The corporate package includes an apartment, a company car, and of course, a highly competitive salary with full benefits. You will not be able to have a dog, a fish, a girlfriend, or even a plant due to the demands of this position, however, if you love engines like I do, and I think you might, you will enter a world where you will never be bored, and you will submerge yourself in the engineering ocean where I believe you are already swimming."

When she finished speaking, Sydney slid a piece of paper cross the desk with the amount of the package that she was proposing and then sat back, crossed her arms, and waited.

Doug sat quietly staring at Syd for what seemed like hours, and as he tried to speak, he found there were no words. His head was swimming, and his tongue felt thick. He began sweating and needed another beer.

"Come with me, I'd like to show you some things that might help you understand the business," Sydney directed as she led him downstairs to her garage. "Let me show you what I do and maybe you will understand the role of the Project Manager better."

As they walked out of her office and down into her garage, Syd's tiny stature seemed to grow as did her excitement upon presenting her private collection of vehicles. His eyes could not believe what he was seeing. The 3,000-square foot garage was spotless, not a crumb on the shiny concrete. Lining the room were some of Sydney's favorites in her collection of automobiles. First on the left was a teal 1958 Chevy Bel Air, four-door hardtop in mint condition. The tires sat with unused tread on a black mat, and the interior was factory perfect.

"My dad was born in 1958, and he bought this beauty in pretty rough shape when he was just old enough to drive. He paid $200 for it, stripped it completely, and restored it to its original condition."

The next car was a black Pontiac 6000STE *Car and Driver's* 1983 Vehicle of the Year.

"This was *THE* car to have the year I was born," Sydney explained. "My dad bought it new to celebrate my birth. He never drove it but stored it all through the years, and I hauled it on the back of a trailer to my shop for display."

After the Pontiac 6000, there was a black 1977 Pontiac Fire Bird Trans-Am made like the iconic car driven by Bert Reynolds in the movie *Smokey and the Bandit*. The next was a bright red 1968 Mustang GT convertible.

"This sweetie belonged to my mom and was brand new when she wrecked it. A car crossed the yellow line and hit her head on one night. She survived, but the car didn't. The insurance company totaled it, so my dad kept it and restored it. She was afraid to drive a stick after the wreck and always had an automatic after that night."

A red and white Ford F150 pick-up truck in its original condition, a 1983 Massey Ferguson tractor, a 1990 Harley Davidson Sportster motorcycle, a 1993 white Ford Bronco identical to the model driven by O.J. Simpson, and a 36-foot Spectre twin engine 500 horsepower fish and ski power boat all lined the walls of the building. The vehicles were parked underneath hanging spotlights that showcased each display, and Doug was overwhelmed and again speechless.

After a few moments, he found his voice.

"Holy Cow, where, how, when? All of these priceless vehicles belonged to your dad?" asked Doug, astonished. "These alone are worth a fortune."

"Each vehicle represented a special memory for Dad. Like I said, the 1958 was to represent his birth, the 6000 was for my birth year, and I think he secretly wanted to drive like Burt Reynolds in the Trans-Am. He loved Ford products, and I believe the Mustang had been bought for himself more so than my mom. He always kept an F150 truck on the farm for hauling things around, and he followed the O.J. Simpson trial every night on the news, so of course he wanted the infamous Ford Bronco to represent that particular event. He once worked as a salesman for Massey Ferguson tractors, and although he was never a rider, he loved Harley Davidson bikes and maybe secretly yearned for the freedom it represented. The twin engine boat mechanics intrigued him, and he bought that one to tear apart and rebuild. This room depicts my dad's love for engines and how they make people, movies, and reality more exciting. The dynamics drove his thirst for design, and he immersed himself in the study of the electronics of engine works. He passed this love of mechanics on to me. And the rest, they say, is history. Let me show you the office and bay area."

As they left the showroom Sydney flipped the lights on to show

Doug a large office with two desktop computers and one laptop.

"This will be your office. Have a seat at the desk, and I can show you how the program works. How computer savvy are you?" Syd asked Doug.

"Not very. However, I use my phone, text...I can use email, and I can find my way around the internet and social media," Doug informed her, and now he wished he had taken more computer classes.

"It won't be a problem. My programs are clear, concise, and straight to the point," Syd explained. "Click on the Engine Wizard Icon in the left corner of the screen."

Doug did as she instructed, and a rotating engine came to life on the computer.

"The column on the left displays the options for each engine. As I research, you can follow my progress daily. You can explore the production steps on screen and how they are bringing the engine to life. My programs will not allow me to continue working on a project if the specs don't match the design outline. I am rejected often during the creative process. Weeks, sometimes months go by before I see a green light on just one small part. It takes patience and focus to walk from one step to the next in the tedious process. You can also find specifications that are required for each project for the day, week, or month. Our communication and updates will be documented so that we can follow the progress of the project and stay within the time frame," Sydney explained carefully and simply so that Doug could follow.

After her demonstration, Doug closed the computer and followed Sydney into the main bay area where engines were secured by chains hanging from the ceiling.

"This is where the magic happens," Sydney said as she walked to one of the sleek, new steel engines. "As the project advances, you will order the parts needed, you will attach and adjust according to specifications until it fires up and hums like a bird."

Sydney made the process sound effortless, but Doug knew better. The decision to accept this position would be based on his love for cars and engines, but in the back of his mind, the idea of working beside this tiny dynamo every day was also a drawing card. He liked her spirit, he liked her drive, and he wanted to be near her every day in any capacity.

Building engines would be the cherry on top.

— CHAPTER 7 —

"When do I start?" Doug asked as his heart raced, and he felt an excitement that had been missing for many years. After sitting down again in the garage office, Doug had thought of a few questions. "Can I ask you something?"

"Absolutely, I expect you have questions," replied Sydney as she pulled out a packet of contracts.

"What happened to your last mechanic? I assume you had someone before, right? Who's been doin' the work for you?" Doug asked.

"I had Cliff. Cliff worked for me until five months ago. He met Lisa on a business trip to London and decided to bring her back with him to America. They fell in love, and things went smoothly for a while. Then one day he thought that bringing her to the garage was a good idea. I found them in the office on the computer watching porn and acting out the video. He no longer works for me, which is why this position is open. Never, ever bring your friends here, not for any reason. Our chance meeting was good timing, and I hope you will accept the offer." Sydney spoke directly and drove her point home. She would not tolerate hanky panky on the job. "I'd like to go over the complete offer before you decide. I would also like to have your signature on the confidentiality agreement if you don't mind." Syd pulled the contracts from the binder and explained each contract.

After carefully reading each sheet, Doug asked, "Let's see if I understand these terms right. I will have an apartment, and it is furnished. If I don't like the furnishings, I can just go out and purchase different furniture on your dollar. I will have not just one but multiple cars to drive at my disposal for business or personal use. I will be paid a very handsome base salary as well as a bonus for each contract, which will be negotiated at the beginning and paid at the end as long as the work comes in on time and meets all specifications? Is this what you are saying?"

Doug looked like a deer staring into high beam headlights.

"You will have two credit cards; one for business purposes for ordering supplies and parts or tools you will need for the project. I will sign off on each purchase or invoice. The other credit card will be your personal card for clothes, food, or whatever you need. I expect honesty and integrity. You will be allocated an amount each month for this card. The business credit card is a black American Express to purchase parts and tools that will be required for each project. They can run into the hundreds of thousands of dollars depending on the project. There are six contracts for you to read, and if you agree, sign and date each one. If you choose to accept my offer, our partnership will be notarized, and our work will begin."

Doug stared at Sydney unable to respond. Was he dreaming? Was she a scam artist? Was this an undercover operation for something illegal? Whatever it was, he wanted in.

"Are you hungry? I'm starving. I think I will go up and make some food. Would you like to read over the contracts here or take them home and think it over? Either is fine; I am not trying to rush you."

Sydney hopped up the stairs in her sneakers, squeaking on the clean floors.

"Feel free to look around as I start cooking, and bring those with you in case you have questions as you read through them. If you would like to have your attorney look them over, I am fine with that as well."

Doug found it funny that Sydney thought he had his own personal lawyer.

Half an hour later, Doug felt confident accepting her offer and realized the kitchen smelled amazing. She had prepared a huge pot of chili, and the aroma made his stomach growl. There were bowls of salad with chunks of cheese, tomatoes, onions, and cucumbers with toasted homemade garlic bread. The table was set with thick, simple white plates, bowls, and heavy glasses for sweet tea.

"She cooks," quipped Doug smiling at Sydney.

"Dissin' the cook is not a good way to impress the boss or begin a new career," teased Sydney. "I take my cooking very seriously, thank you very much," she added. Doug noticed her perfectly straight white teeth when she smiled.

"Well, you are just lucky that I like chili and salad, "he said.

"I love to cook and have missed it since Cliff left. He was a big man with a huge appetite, and it was exciting to watch him eat. It's no fun cooking for one person. There are a dozen or more restaurants within walking distance if you'd rather have a sandwich. My feelings will not be hurt at all if you'd rather eat something else."

Sydney never missed a beat.

"No, no, I'm just fine. You will find I am not a hard man to please, especially when it comes to food." He handed the signed contracts to Sydney. "I would like to accept your offer and join your company, if you really feel that I am qualified."

Doug hoped that she had not already changed her mind.

"I would NOT have offered the position to you if I didn't think you could not do the job. I do not react quickly, nor do I overreact. I don't make emotional decisions and will take hours and maybe days to think about the smallest situation. I never rush, so don't make the mistake of taking me lightly. I say what I mean, and I can be sarcastic at times; that's my attempt at humor. I need my space, and I am a loner at heart, so don't take it personally. There are days I work without speaking, and there are days I shut myself away in my office and research hours on end without a break. I do not need a buddy, I do not need a companion, and I do not need rescuing. I need solitude to focus; it's not personal, it's business. Please respect that. There is no negotiating in business meetings unless I am the negotiator. I am highly intelligent; never forget that, and above all, I am the boss."

Sydney never blinked an eye as she spoke. Her chest rose and fell evenly, and Doug could not stop his eyes from watching as her blouse rose and fell on her chest. It strained at her bra line, and as she caught Doug's eye dropping to that area, she snapped her fingers and said, "Eyes on my face, not my girls. I am not interested in that either. It will behoove you to remember that."

— CHAPTER 8 —

Doug wore jeans and a tee shirt to work on Monday. He called Auto Extreme and turned in his immediate notice over the phone. His Regional Manager was not happy but understood the golden opportunity that had been handed to his best employee. He was happy for Doug and a little envious. When Doug arrived at work, he parked his truck in the back of the building and pushed the code numbers that Sydney had given him. The door clicked, and he was inside. The building was eerily quiet, and he wasn't sure where to start. He didn't have to wonder long when he heard Sydney humming in the garage office.

"Good morning, Doug. You are on time, great beginning. That's nice; please see that you are always on time, if not early. Your work clothes are in your restroom, and coffee is made in your kitchen. Go through your office, and the door is right across the hallway," Sydney stated after realizing Doug looked a little lost.

Doug apparently had not been given the entire tour, as he did not know he had a personal restroom and kitchen. Turning on the lights, Doug found an enormous bathroom with a spacious tile shower, a closet for his clothes where 10 black golf shirts hung with his name monogrammed on the pocket. A patch on the left arm was brilliant red with yellow and white stripes and the company logo. New work boots in the closet, socks in the drawers, and boxer briefs in the closet rounded out his new wardrobe. In each cabinet, there was an array of shaving and personal hygiene items. Syd had thought of everything Doug would need. The room was very masculine in shades of grays mixed with white and black. The kitchen was not as grand as the one upstairs, but there was ample space with a full-size refrigerator stocked with water, sodas, and fruits and vegetables. A microwave, a Keurig coffee maker, and cabinets full of chips, bread, snacks of all types, and even ice cream and yogurt.

"I didn't know what you liked, so I just picked up an array of foods," Syd explained. "This is your domain, and I expect you will change things to the way you like them. Every space must remain clean, which is a feat in itself if you are working with engines, but you will have 10 clean work shirts at all times, so change as frequently as you need. Ron will come by on Friday afternoons to pick up your laundry and provide specialty cleaning to remove the tiniest of shavings from your clothes and linen. A tiny speck of metal can derail a project and cause complete failure making the company lose hundreds of thousands of dollars. Please keep your hands and nails clean and be ready to leave at a moment's notice for a business trip."

Sydney looked at Doug with a twinkle in her eye and said, "I thought you might be a boxer brief kind of guy, so I bought a stash of them. Feel free to exchange them if you want. Any questions?"

"Many," replied Doug. "Like what do I do? Where do I start?"

"Today is orientation to your new environment. You know where most things are in the building. Let's go see your modes of transportation."

Sydney led Doug out to the side parking lot. There were 10 or more vehicles, including a Jeep Cherokee, a lifted Ford F250 that provided side steps Sydney used when she drove it. A BMW SUV, a

Mercedes sportster, a Harley Davidson Indian motorcycle, and a Range Rover rounded out the selection.

"These are company cars that are ours to use for any need. They help as a tax write off," Syd explained as she saw the questioning look in Doug's eyes. "There is a pegboard in your office with two sets of keys for each vehicle. My personal car is Beautiful Betty, who I believe you have met before. It fits me perfectly and feels like my home," Syd explained.

Doug lost focus when she said her car fit her perfectly and thoughts ran through his mind of the day she bent over the fender and worked under the hood. Shaking his head to clear the thoughts he was having, he looked around and appreciated all that she had accomplished in the automobile world.

"Let's take a little walk."

Sydney led Doug down the street a few blocks toward the river as the sun danced brightly on the waves in the winter wind. At the water's edge, they turned left, and the wind whipped sharply around them, sending Sydney's shoulder length auburn hair flying around her face. She laughed as she began spitting long strands of hair from her mouth. There was something naturally feminine about her as she wore little makeup and a simple, sleek hair style. Her only jewelry was a thin silver chain around her neck with a single charm and hoop earrings.

When they reached a three-story red brick building, Doug was ready to go inside to get out of the cold. Syd guided him in and pushed the elevator button for the third floor. As they reached the top floor, Sydney unlocked the second door on the right with her palm identity then instructed Doug to do the same as she reprogrammed the sensors with his features. The apartment faced the street and had a beautiful view of the river beyond.

"Welcome to your new home."

Sydney swiped her arms open and allowed Doug to pass in front of her. This apartment was perfect for a single man. No frills, no fancy furniture, just sturdy, masculine brown and black leathers in a room painted light sand. There was a well-appointed kitchen with new appliances, one large bedroom, and one massive bath that completed the tour. It was better than any home he had ever owned, and he was thankful that she was providing it with his new position.

"This is very nice. I appreciate you lending it to me. I will take good care of your property. I can't say that I am much of a domestic gentleman, but I am neat and keep my things organized. As long as I have a microwave and stove top, I will be fine."

Doug walked through the apartment, appreciating that she had made the effort to buy large furniture to fit a sturdy framed man. The massive California king bed was not only wider but longer and would fit his six-foot-three height without his legs scrunching beneath him at night. The headboard was tall and thick with reading lights mounted on each side. The dark wood dresser and chest would be more than enough to hold his few clothes that he wore when he was not working.

"Thank you so much for this opportunity." He wanted her to know that he was grateful for everything she was doing for him.

"I hope you will enjoy it here. This area has a great night life and you can walk to almost every restaurant and bar in the vicinity. Here are your keys to the building and you will also have a code to unlock your doors if you forget your key, and don't forget you can use your palm access."

Sydney gave him a tour of the balcony and walked with him around the complex to show him the amenities that included a gym, Olympic size pool, and sports center with large screen TVs and internet stations for the tenants.

As they walked back to the garage, Doug couldn't help but notice how Syd kept her distance from him and wondered if that was for professional images or if she really was a loner at heart. Several times during their tour their shoulders brushed, and Sydney immediately pulled away as though she had touched a hot object that burned her skin. He had no idea the sensation it sent through her when they touched. A sensation she wanted to ignore.

Back at the garage, they went inside Doug's office, and Sydney provided him with the codes he needed to begin studying the current project he would be getting to know. She shook his hand and said that he was now officially an employee of SCJ Engineering Enterprises and hoped they would have a long, successful work relationship and build exceptional engines together. Doug secretly hoped for more.

The remainder of the day Doug received emails and texts from Sydney, who was working upstairs in her office. There seemed to be a hundred emails with images, diagrams, and just random thoughts of the new prototype from Sydney. At 7:30, he texted her to let her know he was leaving for the evening. His truck was full of clothes and personal belongs he wanted to take to his new apartment and begin to organize. Sydney texted back to wish him a good night, and he did not see her again before he locked up and left the garage.

The month finished with what Doug felt was little progress, but on the last Friday, he received an email asking him to come up to her office. As he knocked before opening the door, he saw she had her back to the door, working on a computer he had not seen when he first toured her office. She was concentrating on the large diagram of an engine that was staring back at her, and she didn't hear him come in. Her auburn strands were piled on her head and her glasses made her look like a college girl. She was wearing ripped jeans and a Tennessee Vols jersey that had seen better days. He cleared his throat so as not to scare her.

"Good afternoon, Doug, thanks for coming. I'd like to show you something. Come on over so that you can get a closer look." As he leaned over her shoulder, he smelled a light scent of vanilla, and he wanted to nuzzle his nose in her neck. "This is your first week's progress. You made quite a dent in the ground work of PDOB1. I'm pleased with amount of work you produced on its front panel."

Sydney was totally focused on the computer screen.

"Pea Dob 1?" asked Doug. "What the hell does that mean?"

"P is for prototype, DOB is for Doug O'Brian, and 1 is your first project. PDOB1. The next will be PDOB2, and so on. This will be the legal extractive number cycle as we file for patents as they progress. We may find that we have several patents pending at one time. There also may be times that we have to set aside one project to start another that needs to be manufactured faster. It can get hectic at times, and we must be able to multitask and stay focused. Of course, I will be here to hold your hand along the way until you find your bearings and are ready to fly solo.

"Fly solo?" Doug asked nervously.

"Absolutely. My objective is to train you so thoroughly that if I am traveling the projects continue effortlessly without my presence. I can only operate fully functional with a full-scale team, and since you are the only team member on site, we must get you to that level as quickly as possible. Are you up for the challenge? Do you have any questions about what you are seeing? The original file on each program is kept on this main computer in case of a data breached on your file, it is safely stored here in a separate locked program. The information is encoded to be one of the safest made, so we can work fairly with ease, but always, always, always back up several times each day. These prototypes are worth millions of dollars, and I spare no expense to ensure their safety. As you progress in the production of the designs, the insurance increases weekly to update the coverage. You are now worth about one half million insured dollars in your project application due to no activity yet. That will increase even as of this evening at close of business. Depending on your project advancement this week, your design worth will most likely double."

Sydney made this sound so normal, but Doug felt nauseated and completely out of his league. These numbers were foreign to him and just words he had heard all his life but never relevant to him or his work. He was just a mechanic in a national auto supply store. Obviously, his world was changing.

"Have a good night. I will be here filing extensions during the weekend," explained Sydney. Even though Doug's work was coming along smoothly, her research had hit a snag. "Oh, I almost forgot, Monday morning we will be leaving for Chicago. Our plane leaves at 7:30, so be here at 6:00 sharp. It's frigid this time of year in Chicago, so bring heavy clothes. If you've never been to the Windy City, you will know why it is named that in about two-point-five seconds after we get off the plane."

"Chicago? As in Illinois?" asked Doug. He had never been to Chicago; he had never even flown on a plane, but he didn't want Sydney to know this bit of information. She already thought he was just a stupid country boy. Why should he prove that point to her? He didn't even have clothes to wear and had no idea what to pack. Should he ask if she wanted him to wear a suit, casual clothes, or his work clothes? Would he sound ridiculous asking such a question? How could he phrase it so that he would not sound green behind the ears?

"What will we be doing in Chicago?" Doug thought this might sound less nervous.

"We will be meeting with Matthew Daniels, who was in charge of the meeting I had to postpone the day I met you. He is one of our leading sponsors and will be investing $10 million in the project you are now building. We had a Skype conference earlier this week, and I apologize for not including you. I have been working alone for a while and completely forgot that you were downstairs working. I will make sure you are included in all meetings forward."

Sydney never blinked as she explained the process to Doug.

"Glad I am so easy to forget," grinned Doug, as he tried to loosen Sydney's demeanor. It did not work.

Just to give Doug some background information, Syd explained, "Matt and I have a long history, and he believes in me. He gave me support when no one else would even take a look at my designs. He invested in me when no one gave me a second thought, and he is one of the main reasons my engine designs have become internationally accepted. I owe him a lot, and I never forget those who gave me a boost on my way into the male career in planes, trains, and automobiles. One thing you will learn in this business is to always remain faithful to those who help you, and don't waste your time on those who do not, and never turn your back on either. Matt is one person I completely trust. After we meet with his team, we will tour the plant, and you will have a much clearer idea where your work goes after it leaves our garage. No suits with Matt, just shirts and tie during the day meeting, and then jeans and very warm sweaters for the nights. We will return on Thursday and work both Saturday and Sunday next week, so if you have plans, please cancel them." Sydney was very direct.

"Do you ever lighten up?" Doug asked. He didn't mind that she was all business, but a little personality in the mix would be nice.

"Doug, I am not here to be nice or lighten up or have fun. I thought I made myself clear on this," Sydney barked. "I am here to work, and if you are looking for a playground buddy, maybe you are in the wrong job. There is nothing light about my work. It is demanding, draining, and on a good day, it is downright overwhelming. If I ever 'lighten up,' my competitors will target me and swoop in for the kill. My business will be torn to shreds, my career will be over as well as yours; my talent, my ingenuity, my hard work, all for nothing, and I will never allow that to happen. So, no Doug, I cannot ever lighten up. I cannot afford that, and you cannot afford that either. If we are to be a team, it will serve you to remove the term 'lighten up' from your vocabulary."

"You obviously passed Bitch 101 at Harvard with flying colors," Doug snapped back at Sydney. He was tired, hungry, and ready to go to his apartment for the weekend. A cold beer and pizza had his name on it and he was eager to get there.

"You say I am a bitch, fine. If I were a man, I would be aggressive, industrious, and competitive. But since I am a woman, I am a bitch. Be sure to let me know if working for a bitch bothers you too much. You might appreciate this bitch once you look at your direct deposit, which I am assuming is more than you have ever had deposited at one time. I hired you from behind an auto supply counter; I am paying you a very handsome salary, providing you with an apartment, your choice of cars, and unlimited use of credit cards, and offering you a chance at a life you would never know without this opportunity. Do not forget that."

Sydney was tired and irritable.

"I was not homeless when we met. I was happy and working in a job I enjoyed. Don't treat me like I am some project of yours. You are paying me a wonderful salary and offering me the opportunity of a lifetime, I get that. But I will not work with an uppity, rude boss—male or female, and you do not need to forget that. Treat me with respect, or build your own PSCJ1 engine."

Doug walked out of her office and slammed the door. He immediately chose the keys to the Mercedes off the key board, left the garage, and headed for the mall where he had to go shopping for Monday's trip, if he still had a job.

Her head was aching, and she needed a glass of wine. Sydney felt bad that she had snapped at Doug. When he leaned over, he was too close, and he smelled good even after a day working in the bay. All week, those light blue eyes stared through her. He made her feel naked, and when they had a conversation, her palms sweated. If she could just keep him at a distance, there would be no problems, but she couldn't, and his effect on her could not always cause her to snap like this. Why on Earth would she react this way to Doug? She had never been attracted to her employees or even her coworkers, not Cliff, not even Matt, and he was an attractive man. She shut her computer down and decided it was a good time to pour that glass of wine.

— CHAPTER 9 —

Monday morning, Doug arrived at 6:00 with his bag packed and was ready to fly. Syd drove the Range Rover to the airport and checked it in the parking garage for the duration of their trip. They picked up tickets at the kiosk and checked their bags, ready to board the plane. The conversation from Friday had not been mentioned, and neither wanted to revisit it. Sydney seemed more relaxed and looked forward to seeing her friend Matt. Doug had never flown and followed Sydney to the waiting area, not knowing what was in store on his inaugural flight. He tried to hide his nervousness from Sydney, but she knew he was a new passenger.

As the plane left the runway, Doug's stomach felt queasy, but that subsided once they reached top altitude. He was enjoying the flight, and Sydney had given him the window seat. Their first-class tickets afforded plenty of room for his long legs to stretch, and when he looked over at Syd, she was asleep. He stared at her for a long while and watched as her breasts would rise and fall a few times when she breathed in gently then softly exhaled. Auburn feathers framed her face and her lashes fluttered from time to time, indicating that she was dreaming. He wanted to touch her lips and run this thumb across her smooth skin. He wanted to know her; he wanted to touch her, and other thoughts crossed his mind as he watched her sleep. But Syd had made it perfectly clear that she had no interest in a personal relationship with anyone. Was she an iron woman? Did she have a softer inside, or was her heart made of steel? Could she love anyone? Was her only passion for the engines that had no beating heart?

As Doug watched her sleeping, she stirred slightly, opened her eyes, and met his gaze. For a moment, time stood still; she did not turn away but held his gaze. The fire in her eyes matched the softness of the lashes framing them, and for just a second, they were equals and not boss and employee. They were two adults who appreciated each other and could have met anywhere. Sydney blinked, and the moment passed. It had been there, but no longer, and now the plane was descending and it was time to unload.

Meeting Matthew Daniels was quite an experience for Doug. He swept Sydney up in arms and swung her around in a circle when they met. It was obvious they had a past. Sydney became a completely different person around Matt. She was casual, relaxed, and almost playful. Matt shook Doug's hand vigorously but not in a showy fake way. It was apparent that he was in charge of his environment and even Sydney seemed dazed in his presence. She laughed freely, and she looped her arm in his while walking through the airport corridor. Doug felt a sharp stab of jealousy and wondered if he would be the third wheel during this trip.

After claiming their bags, Matt drove them to the hotel, so they could check into their rooms. The hotel was luxurious and their rooms were on the top floor and each had a suite. After depositing Doug at his door, Matt and Sydney walked away in the direction of her room as any everyday couple. He instructed Doug to meet them at the restaurant in the lobby for lunch at noon, and after, they would go to the conference room on the second floor for the presentation at 2:00.

Doug changed into a light blue oxford shirt and tie he had

bought with new navy slacks. Since business meetings and travel were new to him, he needed to purchase socks and shoes, belts, ties, shirts, and slacks. The amount he spent was more than he had spent on clothes in his life, and he felt guilty for using his corporate credit card. Doug came out of his room just in time to meet Sydney at the elevator, and he knew he had made the right choice by the look in her eyes. She approved of his corporate attire, and her nod told him so.

"You clean up pretty nicely, Mr. O'Brian," said Sydney with a slight smile.

Matthew Daniels was at the restaurant waiting for them and had ordered lunch drinks for everyone. Their meal conversation was light, and Doug learned more about Sydney as he listened to the two reminiscing about family, college, and their social history. They included Doug in the conversation, and Matt seemed genuinely interested in his background and why he became interested in mechanics. Sydney looked surprised when she learned that Doug had attended college at the University of Georgia but dropped out in his final year when his father became ill and his family needed him to move back home to help with finances. Doug had returned home to work so that his mother could take a leave of absence from her nursing job to care for his dad during chemotherapy. That was when he went to work at a local auto supply chain and had worked for the company since that time. Sydney was impressed that he would put his own education aside to move back home and care for his family. To Syd, this displayed true character and selflessness. In the years that followed, Doug wanted to complete his degree in business in night classes but never did. He was promoted to manager at the parts store and didn't enroll in another college class.

At 2:00, Matt's team assembled, which comprised of himself, the CEO of Daniels International, Charles Lee, CFO of both domestic and international branches, Robert Hayden, Chief of

Engine Design, and six other men of various positions. Sydney was the only female present. They were all nice but completely stoned face. She looked breathtaking in a black pencil skirt just short enough to show off her shapely legs, a pale blue silk blouse with a simple set of pearls around her neck. She wore pearl earrings and a matching pearl bracelet with very little makeup. Her hair was pulled back in a chignon, and her matching black jacket created the professional look she desired. Her black high heels made Doug's heart race, and he could only imagine taking them off for her. As Matthew introduced Sydney to the room of men, it was obvious they respected her work, and she commanded her audience. Syd introduced Doug as her new Production Manager and explained that he would be answering any questions after the presentation of the prototype. She had failed to mention this to him and immediately a lump formed in his throat.

Doug sat spellbound as Sydney worked her magic on the men in the room. She gave each person a tablet and explained the preloaded prototype they would see as they logged in. Her information was clear and simple but extremely complicated. Without blinking, each pair of eyes was fixated on her presentation, and she knew exactly how to excite them in their own field of typically boring engine design. She brought enthusiasm, passion, and complete confidence as she walked around the room with animated gestures and gave examples of what lay ahead with the success of the engine.

Forty-five minutes later, the lights brightened, and she announced that she and Doug would answer 15 minutes of questions. As the questions began Doug was surprised that each one she directed to him was one to which he knew the answer. The nervousness faded as he answered each with more confidence, and his momentum increased with each correct answer. At the end of the presentation, they all shook his hand and said that Sydney had indeed found a competent counterpart for her designs. Time flew by, and before they knew it, the meeting was over, and everyone left feeling quite accomplished.

Outside the conference room, Sydney gave Matt a hug and told him to text her later before dinner. In the elevator, Sydney asked Doug if he would mind stopping by her room for a few moments to go over a few details. Doug worried that he had made some mistakes, but as they came into her suite, Sydney immediately took off her shoes and kicked them across the room. She had ordered a bottle of champagne on ice with a platter of strawberries, grapes, crackers, and cheese on a rolling cart covered with a white linen tablecloth.

"You can take off your tie now if you like," Sydney said, noticing Doug tugging at his collar. He loosened his tie as she poured them both a glass of bubbling champagne. She brought the tray over to the couch and placed it between them as she gave him his flute filled with the clear liquid. Doug preferred beer but would take whatever she offered him. He was parched. Syd tucked her legs underneath her and looked at Doug as she said, "Thank you, Doug. We did it."

"Did what?" asked Doug, still unclear of what they had really accomplished in the meeting.

"Matt's company just paid 10 million dollars to develop and produce the PDOB1. Soon your engine will be shipped to companies across the world, and Daniels International will partner with us to build them for their emergency vehicles. In these vehicles, speed and accuracy is imperative to provide patient transportation to hospitals that are sometimes hours and many miles away. I believe this belongs to you," as she handed Doug a thick bound instruction manual with an envelope tucked inside the cover. "You just earned half of your first commission."

Sydney handed Doug a check in the amount of $50,000.

"Congratulations on a great job. I couldn't have accomplished this without you," she added ss she held her glass up to his, and they clinked in celebration.

An empty bottle and half eaten tray of strawberries and cheese, later they were talking like old friends. Doug wanted to reach over and touch her hand or caress her arm, but he didn't dare. Sydney stood and told Doug she needed a nap and a shower, and they were meeting Matt at 8:00 for dinner. This was Doug's cue to leave, as she was already yawning when she led him to the door.

Matt, Robert, Sydney, and Doug drove to Gibson's, the star famed restaurant where they enjoyed a great meal of lobster, steak, and more side dishes than Doug had ever seen. It was delicious, and the food continued to appear at their table course after course. Beer and wine flowed freely, and everyone celebrated their accomplishment. They all looked forward to the launch of the new project in six weeks.

Sydney was having a great night as she laughed effortlessly and was more at ease than Doug had seen so far. Matt sat with his arm draped over her shoulder at times and the back of her chair at other times. It was obvious that their friendship ran deep, and Doug wondered just well they knew each other. After dinner, the foursome went to the rooftop deck to dance and continue celebrating. Doug went to the bar to get beer, and when he returned Sydney and Matt were on the dance floor having a great time. After a few dances, Matt and Robert went in search of new dance partners, leaving Doug and Sydney alone at their table.

"You and Matt have known each other a long time, haven't you?" asked Doug even though he had been watching them all day and could see they were old friends, if not more.

"Yes, we go way back. His family and mine were great friends. We attended Harvard at the same time, and when I went to MIT, he accepted a fellowship at Oxford for two years. He traveled the globe, living the high life until his daddy made him return home to settle down and get serious about a career. In the meantime, I was working, brainstorming, and scratching my way through the male dominated corporate world of automobiles and finance. By the time I designed my first accelerated engine prototype, he had made enough money to invest in my dream. And the rest, as they say, is history. We have had our ups and downs over the years, but we stay close. He is like the brother I always wanted but never had. The best part of our relationship is that we respect one another for what we bring to the table. Matt is a great guy," Sydney explained.

"Are you sure you're not a couple?" Doug asked, pleading inside for her to say no.

"Oh God no," exclaimed Sydney. "I know Matt way too well for that. When I say he is a great guy, I mean he is a great friend, a great business partner, but a great life partner? Absolutely not. We would drive each other crazy. Matt likes women, a lot. He is in the field for the money and has made a lot of it—for both of us—but he doesn't have the passion I have for an engine. He can't see the fine lines and feel the smooth finish of the steel. He can't run his fingers across the spectrum and feel a barb or experience the excitement when the pistons are firing, and it comes to life. When the engine roars and it performs like an iconic band, Matt feels nothing. All he hears is the *cha-ching* of the money he is making. Then he gets excited."

"Would you like to dance?" Doug asked when a slow song began. And before she could object, he took her hand and led Sydney to the dance floor and pulled her into his arms as he looked into her eyes. His eyes mesmerized her, and it made her feel small as her legs became weak. Doug never took his eyes from hers as the music played. He pulled her closer as their torsos melted into one, and the desire for her became unbearable. The music was soft as they moved together, and Doug caressed Sydney's back with one hand while holding her hand in the other. As she raised her face to his, he was so close to kissing her.

"Hey guys, we're back," announced Matt. "We didn't find any suitable ladies. We're heading back to the hotel. We have a busy day ahead tomorrow when we tour the plant. Wear comfortable shoes, as we will be walking quite a bit. Doug, I think you will really enjoy seeing what we are going to do to your first project."

Doug and Sydney pulled apart as the four walked toward the elevator ready to leave.

They arrived back at the hotel and the magic spell was broken. And just like that: Sydney was back in work mode.

"Goodnight, Doug," Sydney yawned. "See you at 7:00 sharp. Tomorrow is casual day. It will be great. I think you will really be impressed."

The next two days were a whirlwind of meetings, diagramming blueprints, and learning how they would function as one team. Doug liked Matt and Robert and knew he would learn a lot from them. They were eager to answer any of his questions and give feedback on how to improve on techniques to use in future projects. The trip had been a success and hopefully the first of many to come.

— CHAPTER 10 —

After Sydney and Doug returned to the garage, their days were long and the work intense. On more than one occasion, Sydney snapped, and Doug retorted. Doug became so outraged at one point that he left for the day and didn't return to the garage but went to the local pub for beer. One week turned into two, and tensions were mounting with the development of PDOB1.

On a Thursday night, the temperature had plummeted to 22 degrees, and the heating element in the bay was not working correctly. The cold atmosphere affected the performance of the project, and Doug was beyond frustrated. He had walked out to make some coffee and take a break when Sydney came bounding down the stairs in her sock feet, cashmere sweater, and stretchy leggings. As Doug was stepping out of the bay into the garage, Sydney slid and almost ran into him, causing him to splash hot coffee on his shirt and chest.

"God, Syd, watch where you are going, you probably burned the hair off my chest," Doug said sharply.

"Well, this wouldn't happen if you had on your thicker work shirt like you should," Sydney snapped back.

"I took it off because it had grease on it because the damn

temperature is so cold in the bay, and the grease is getting thick on the engine," Doug fumed. He had changed into a pair of jeans and a crisp white t-shirt. The white shirt was now wet and brown from his coffee.

Sydney walked over to the Trans Am and opened the trunk.

"Here put this on," Sydney said as she threw a shirt at him. "I keep boxes of extra clothes around for times like this."

Before Doug knew what happened, he jerked the stained shirt off and in a flash grabbed Sydney by her wrists and pushed her backwards onto the hood of the Trans Am. Picking her up and sitting her firmly on the hood of the car he took her face in his hands and watching her every move, kissed her bottom lip. The second time he lightly tugged her lip with his teeth, and she parted her lips with a soft groan. Doug took the opportunity and gently probed her mouth open as she accepted his kiss.

He held her face firmly in his hands and never closed his eyes. He wanted to see her, kiss her, feel her, and more than anything, he wanted her to see him. As the kisses became harder and more intense, he lifted her sweater over her arms, ran his hand under her camisole and massaged her breasts gently. Sydney let out a groan as he pulled both her arms behind her back as he bit her soft skin gently. Circling the tender brown sections, he blew out cold breath and watch them hardened immediately.

As he pushed Sydney onto the hood of the car, she threw her head back and arched her back upward when he ran his tongue down her stomach. With one hand Doug removed her leggings and pulled her hips toward him, gently massaging her in circles. Doug lifted her hips and pulled her legs around him causing her to gasp. Gently at first, then harder, she clinched her legs around his hips, wanting his fullness inside her as deeply as possible. She couldn't get enough of him, and he couldn't go fast enough. Syd was pushing against the car's hood for leverage, and Doug was pushing toward her as hard as possible with all of his might as sweat rolled down his chest.

Sydney let out a scream of delight as Doug felt the warmth of his excitement overcome them both and not once did his eyes leave hers. Syd lowered her back onto the car as Doug felt his legs begin to tremble. It was great; no, it was better than great, just as he knew it would be.

Once she gained her senses, Sydney could not imagine why she had let this happen. How could she be so irresponsible? She had never allowed herself to become involved with her employees, not her coworkers nor any of her friends. After a moment, Doug backed away, and Syd grabbed her clothes in her arms then ran up the stairs to her apartment. She didn't realize that tears were streaming down her cheeks until she reached her bedroom where she felt like her heart was pounding out of her chest.

Quickly locking her door, Syd ran into her bathroom and ran hot steaming water to take a shower. She sat on the big seat in her shower and held her face in her hands while she cried. For at least 10 minutes, Sydney cried until there were no more tears. After scrubbing her skin until she felt all of Doug was removed from her and the water was cold, only then did Syd wrap her hair in a towel and tuck her naked body under the covers in her big comfortable bed and sleep...

She was dreaming, dreaming that she was running; faster and faster, she tried to run, but the harder she ran, the less ground she was covering. She began to scream. She screamed and screamed until she awoke to realize what she thought was her screaming was actually her doorbell. Syd looked over at her clock to see that it was 9:30 a.m. Who was at her door and ringing her door bell? She was naked and cold and had a headache. She had slept fitfully all night. After grabbing her robe and pulling on wool socks, Syd went to the door and asked who was there.

"It's me Syd," said Doug. "Can I come in?"

"Oh, sorry Doug, I am just getting out of the shower," Sydney lied. "I'll be down in a bit. Give me 15 minutes to dry my hair," replied Syd in a raspy voice. Her head was pounding, and she needed hot coffee and aspirin.

Wearing a dark blue pair of dress jeans and a heavy teal cashmere sweater, Sydney came into Doug's office holding a soft leather brief bag. It was dark brown with sturdy handles and a shoulder strap.

"This is for your documents on the PDOB2 with plenty of room for safekeeping of our new presentation proposal. We will leave for Seattle on Friday. It will be cold and rainy, so pack accordingly. Our plane leaves at 5:15 Friday morning. Please meet me here at 4:00, so that we can get through security. We will stop in Atlanta and also in Dallas."

Sydney pulled her hair behind her ears, and Doug could see that she was all business again and had no intention of talking about their encounter the night before.

"Sydney," Doug began, but she cut him off before he could say anymore. She sensed that he wanted to talk about it but she wasn't ready yet or if ever.

"I am beginning research on a four-facet high powered engine fueled by diesel and electricity. It needs to exceed speeds of 70 miles per hour, but it will only be used within the Heiss-North Industries. Heiss-North is a city bus builder. They will need 150 engines built and want us to pitch the product. Our trip to Seattle will introduce the requirements I will be researching as well as output and efficiency. This is not as exciting as the PDOB1 but will be implemented into the green movement in Seattle and help the environment immensely by trading the gasoline powered buses that Heiss is now producing."

Sydney was immersed in her explanation of the purpose of their trip when Doug interrupted her.

"You are so beautiful." Doug looked at her deeply and never blinked.

Sydney closed her eyes for a moment.

"You are my employee, Doug, I am the business owner, and we crossed the line. It was a huge mistake; one that I have never made and will not make again. Please respect that decision," Sydney stated flatly.

"If you don't mind, I will not remember it as a mistake, but as an amazing experience. I will respect your decision, but I will not forget last night."

Doug turned and walked into his office kitchen for a second mug of coffee.

"I will see you on Friday; I am going to take off for the next two days. I will be researching while I am on the road. You can reach me by cell if you need me," Sydney told Doug but offered no explanation as to where she would be going. "Have a productive couple of days, and I will meet you here Friday morning. Please don't be late," Sydney said over her shoulder as she walked out.

"I am never late, or maybe you haven't noticed," Doug mumbled under his breath.

Sydney needed a break. She needed to clear her thoughts. Her head was fuzzy, and she could not stop thinking of the passion that so quickly overtook them. Doug's bright blue eyes bore into hers, and he was so intent on pleasing her. Their entire passionate encounter could not have taken more than 15 minutes but it made her weak rethinking it. It was not just a chance hook-up; they had made love—

No, they didn't make love, they had sex; pure unbridled sex. There was no love between them, and there would never be. Love was not in the cards for Syd. She would never find true love or marry or have a family. Her family was her business, and she had deliberately made that decision so that she could devote every moment to the designs that she produced. This building, these walls, these cars were her lifeblood, and she would not allow any person or feelings to come before or between it. A few days away from Doug was just what she needed to get back on track.

— CHAPTER 11 —

The grave where her parents were buried was in a perpetual cemetery. It was kept immaculately clean and decorated by a grounds crew where Sydney always thought it felt peaceful and serene. Not often, but about twice each year, Syd would change out the flowers in the vase that stood in the center of a marker bearing her father's name on the left and her mother's on the right. It seemed like a lifetime ago that she was their only child and they adored her.

Sydney had been given the best of everything; a wonderful home, land to keep horses to ride as well as dogs, so many dogs, with fields where she could run and play. Sydney loved school and especially math and reading. She aced every accelerated test and was recommended for private school. She attended a girls' school for both middle and high school before venturing north first to Knoxville then on to Harvard. Syd had traveled to cities all over the world to study history and experience life first hand in the geographical subject matter. By the time Sydney graduated high school, she was fluent in Spanish, German, French, and Mandarin. She took her school work seriously and never caused her parents any worry. Their personal problems were enough to keep her from causing any problems in their home. A light heart attack had scared her dad into making better health choices, and by the time she went away to college he had stopped drinking completely, and things were looking up in her parents' relationship. Her mother had started coming back home more often, and the two seemed to be getting along better. The three were always close, and she missed them together as a family.

Sydney was a daddy's girl at heart, and his wisdom still guided her every day. She heard his voice in her business transactions constantly guiding her, and it was his warnings that were telling her not to get involved with a coworker or employee. He always taught her that if she wanted to make her mark in life, then work must be priority. She must stay focused, razor sharp, and remain impersonal. Sydney didn't learn things like playing with dolls, dancing, or wearing makeup. When her mom left, Syd was just beginning to need feminine guidance, but instead, her father had provided the masculine side of her questions. Her mother had always kept their home beautifully decorated, always immaculate and ready to entertain at a moment's notice. However, her dad had been the one in the stands when Sydney played softball and taught her to ride a motorcycle. Claire had a green thumb and grew vivid hydrangeas and iris plants in bright colors, and in the spring, magazine photographers sought her out to write articles on her beautifully landscaped yard and flower garden. Their home had appeared in *Southern Home and Garden* magazine with Claire as the mastermind, creating elegant décor throughout and offering advice on ways to create a calming and welcoming sanctuary to call home after work and school. Sydney didn't inherit her mother's desire to be a stay at home mom, but she loved to decorate and create a warm welcome atmosphere in her own home.

These early childhood memories caused Syd to miss them both so much. After their separation, it became harder for her to imagine a happy home, but over the years she came to understand how addiction played into family dynamics. Once her father stopped drinking, he focused more on her mother and tried to reestablish their relationship to where it once had been. They both loved her very much and made certain she had everything she needed to be successful in her life. She still needed their advice from time to time, and today was certainly one of those times. She had crossed the professional line with Doug. Syd messed it all up by lying across a car and allowing Doug break her own cardinal rule.

After visiting the cemetery, Syd drove the short distance to her childhood farm, and it brought tears to her eyes as she watched children and puppies play in her front yard. The stately home was well kept, and the family looked happy as she slowed her car to watch for a moment. Her memories of happy days and her own childhood caused loneliness and regret to sweep in and take over her mood. Why did she choose this life? Was she making her mark? Did anyone even care if she designed the fastest, most efficient engines in the world? Was she missing out by not settling down with a partner and having a family?

Sydney shook her head.

Of course, this was her dream; it was her daddy's dream as well. He died early at only 65, and her mother five years later, neither of them living out a very long life. But Sydney was living the dream, right? As long as she was producing engines, her father was still alive and very much living his dream through her. It was the least she could do for him after all he had poured into her education and training year after year until cancer snuffed out his life way too early.

A horn beeped behind Sydney to prod her into moving forward. She was now officially in a funk. She phoned her uncle to let them know she was in town and would love to stop by for a visit. She was happy to hear that he was staying busy after his retirement and beginning to make plans to travel and enjoy the second half of his life. After stuffing herself with her aunt's wonderful home cooking, Sydney spent the next day with her cousin, who was living his dream as a professor, and his enthusiasm of a life of solitude was proof that one could love their chosen life and have no family or love interest. He convinced Sydney that his life was full and satisfying with lots of friends and coworkers with whom he regularly socialized and traveled to exciting cities and foreign countries. His calendar was constantly full, and he was never alone. As a result he said he never felt lonely.

Sydney had no real friends and only one coworker and was feeling lonely for the first time in several years. Syd thought maybe she should get a dog to keep her company. But a dog was difficult to travel with, and she didn't want to use a boarding house or kennel. Surely this feeling would pass; it always did. But there was something different this time. She was actually questioning the decisions she had made for her life years before. Was she depressed? Had she wasted many years trying to prove something? And if so, to whom? Was she softening regarding the boundaries she had set for herself? Or perhaps she was just softening in her old age.

"That's just ridiculous," Sydney scolded herself. "I am happy and not lonely. I will get a dog...or a cat...or a fish...or something... and that will be that."

— CHAPTER 12 —

On Friday morning, Sydney met Doug at the garage refreshed and ready to tackle a new project by beginning their trip to Seattle. After settling in their first-class seats, Doug noticed that Syd had pushed her earbuds in and was already in her world of research. A few minutes later, he glanced at the screen she was reading and realized it was in a foreign language. Not wanting to startle her, Doug lightly touched her arm to gain her attention, and his stomach fluttered at the softness of her skin.

"What language is that?" asked Doug not recognizing any of the words.

"It's German. The North-Heiss Industry is based in Frankfurt, and their management team does not speak English. The specifications manual is written in their native language, and there is not an English translation," Sydney explained.

"I didn't know you speak German. Do you speak other languages?" Doug asked impressed.

"I speak German, Spanish, French, Italian, and Mandarin," Sydney stated matter of factly. She made it sound like she was reading a simple meatloaf recipe.

"You never fail to impress me, Sydney James. Will you always intrigue me? Is there no end to your surprises?" Doug wanted to know everything about her.

"The languages have become useful to me over the years and are more accurate than using a translator. I don't trust facts and figures getting lost during translations. I can't afford a mistake that could cost us millions of dollars in a product."

As the plane landed in the Atlanta Hartsfield Airport, Doug was amazed at the city within the airport terminal. He had never seen anything like it and was nervous as he became part of the chaos. Doug wondered if he would ever become accustomed to this jet setting lifestyle.

Their time was tight as Doug and Syd practically ran from the Southwest plane they had just departed to board the Delta that would fly them first to Dallas then on to Seattle. There was no layover, just an exchanging of planes. Perhaps he would come back one day and take a leisurely walk through the world's largest airport. He had come a long way in a short time in so many ways in his life and found it all fascinating.

After settling in their expansive seats, Sydney reclined her seat back to take a nap.

"Sydney, will you talk to me?" Doug asked quietly. His thumb gently pushed her bangs out of her eyes and looked at her as she was relaxing. "Won't you let me in?" He then realized she was already fast asleep.

Seattle loomed ahead, and the lights were brilliant underneath the wings of the plane. He could see the space needle and was hoping to take a tour during their visit. Doug remembered reading about it in high school and had always wanted to see it. In the darkness it was hard to imagine the city in the daylight and Doug looked forward to the next day's agenda.

Sydney woke as the plane descended and said she was hungry. After claiming their bags and hailing a taxi, they made their way to the hotel. Sleeker and much taller than the Chicago hotel, Doug stood by Syd as she pushed the button to the top floor as it lit "23." She always booked close to the top floor because it gave the best views of the cities below. The top floor was usually close to a restaurant or bar and often provided a rooftop deck for dancing and relaxing. As Doug took his key card and entered the room, he noticed an adjoining door to Sydney's suite and wondered if he might have a chance to talk with her during this trip.

"Let's meet in two hours for dinner," suggested Sydney. "I need a shower."

"Sure, I'll be ready. What's the dress for dinner?" asked Doug.

"Business casual, no tie for tonight," said Sydney. She knew he would need to dress more professionally for the entire day of meetings the next day.

After an amazing meal of white fish and chips with a specialty tarter glaze, both Sydney and Doug slumped back in their seats barely able to breathe.

As he looked over at the dessert cart, Doug rolled his eyes back.

"I have no idea what that dessert is but I'm game. Can we share one? I'm pretty stuffed," Doug said with a groan as he patted his stomach.

"Sure, we can get two spoons. The servings here are enormous, so there will be plenty."

Sydney instructed the server to bring one dessert, so they could share.

Watching her gently scoop out the delicious coffee flavored cream and unconsciously twirl the spoon around on her tongue drove him crazy. He wanted his arms around her like nothing he had ever felt before. The music was a jazz band, which was not Doug's favorite, but a slow romantic song began, and he took her hand and led her to the dance floor just beyond the dinner tables. Sydney hesitated but didn't resist and allowed him to pull her gently into his arms.

"I need to talk to you about this, Doug," Sydney said.

"Shshsh, don't talk now. Just let me hold you for a moment. I have been having dreams of a second dance with you ever since we left Chicago."

Doug closed his eyes and held her close.

"Doug, we can't do this. It isn't in the cards for me, and my personal bio doesn't have room for an affair with my employee. I have never allowed myself this luxury, and I can't now," Sydney said matter of factly. "It was a mistake I can't afford to make again."

"Syd, I don't want to have an affair with you. I want you, all of you. I want your body, and I want your heart. I want to work with you every day, and I want to see you every night. I'm not very experienced in the field of love, and I've only had one serious relationship, but I think I'm falling in love with you," Doug whispered. "Please don't say anything, just dance with me, and let me touch you."

As they danced Doug smelled the freshness of Sydney's hair and his nose inched down her neck and onto her shoulder. He looked deep into her eyes, and she felt a stirring deep in her soul and her body ached for him. The dance ended, but they continued to hold each other and sway like no one was watching. Doug led Sydney to the hallway to catch the elevator down to their suites, and Sydney didn't pull away from his protective arm around her waist.

As the elevator door shut, Doug turned and pinned Sydney to the wall as he lifted her hips up to him. She locked her legs around him, and he held her face in both his hands as he looked deep into her eyes and took possession of her mouth. Her hands immediately wrapped around his shoulders and dug into his soft brown hair. Neither of them closed their eyes, but wanted to see every moment of this kiss.

After Sydney took her room key from her pocket, Doug picked her up and laid her gently across the massive king sized bed. He slowly and gently slid her top from her shoulders and began kissing her neck and throat. He had dreamt of his tongue looping around the delicate necklace that fell into the crevice at her throat. Doug's hand and mouth found her breasts and as he circled them with his tongue; they hardened under his touch until she groaned, and Syd dug her nails into his shoulders.

As Doug slowly removed her pants, he slid his fingers inside the lacy panties she was wearing, and she begged him to explore deeper. As he undressed standing before her, she admired his large frame, so tall and muscular. It was obvious he worked with his hands, arms, and shoulders by their size and shape. Doug's body was not one that boasted hours at the gym but instead working long hard hours using muscles that produced something of worth.

Doug sat with his legs crisscrossed on the bed and pulled Syd's tiny frame on top on his lap facing him. He kissed her long and hard, but tender and gently at the same time. She wrapped her legs around his waist as he took control of her motions in a rhythm matching his. Together, they explored love making, reaching heights neither had experienced before. Syd rolled her eyes back in her head as Doug's hands found places that she had only imagined being touched by anyone. She arched her back as he kissed first her stomach and downward, sending chills up her spine. He gently lifted her and turned her away from him while keeping her on his lap.

As they found pleasure again and again in different positions, Sydney leaned back into him and thought she would scream as the same intense pleasure found her over and over. His hands were large and smooth and talented. He brought her to heights she had never imagined with his entire body, hands, and tongue Sydney thought she would surely explode into a million little pieces. They fell back on the bed completely exhausted but satisfied and ready to sleep.

"Oh God, Doug, how can you make me feel like this?" Sydney could barely breathe as she whispered his name.

"Let me love you, Sydney. Let me inside your heart, and I will never hurt you. This is more than an affair to me. I want to love every part of you, inside and out. I have never felt like this before," Doug said as sweat formed on his brow. He watched her, waiting for a response as she fell into a peaceful sleep.

They remained in her bed that night, and Sydney woke to Doug kissing her as they spooned in the early hours of dawn. The heavy comforter covered his head as he scooted downward and began kissing the inside of her thighs. Sydney rolled over on her back, kicked the covers off so that he could breathe, and wrapped her legs around his head. After pure joy lasted for much too short a time, Doug ran a bath in the giant Jacuzzi tub and carried Syd's warm naked body to the bubbles. As she enjoyed the swirling water jetting around her, she relaxed backward and found him standing above her. Her hands ran up his firm legs and circled his rock-hard torso before finding him with her lips. The sweet taste of him caused her to tremble, and he knelt before her to allow her to reach all of him. As he held her hair and head, his eyes never left hers, and she watched closely as she pleased him to the point of exploding. He sank into the water beside her, and she sat on his lap as he washed her entire body with bubbles and bath soaps.

Breakfast was quick, and soon both Doug and Sydney were dressed and prepared for the day's meetings with George Von Heissleman. Sydney updated Doug on the engine Heissleman wanted to build for his company. Heiss, known by his competitors, was an environmental strategist on the city bus market. Seattle was attempting to become one of the nation's top ten cleanest cities, and its public transportation system needed upgrading to make this happen. The city government had awarded the bid to Heiss, and now his company needed to find the most economically clean engine to run the buses. Sydney had gone over the specification manual with a fine-tooth comb and felt that she had educated herself on how she and Doug needed to proceed. She had poured over the fine print in the spec pages and knew how much it would cost to produce, how much time they needed, and precisely when the prototype could be released for approval.

Four hours later, Doug was once again amazed at her prowess in handling the German executives. Her language was flawless and no interpreters were needed for their CEO and management team. The hotel had provided earbuds for them to translate into English for her presentation, and he watched her closely as again she worked the room and had the men eating out of her hands. The contract was now hers, and she and Doug had secured another project to begin.

After the meeting ended, Doug and Sydney toured the Pike Place Market and watched the boats come into Elliot Bay with their fish catch of the day. They were amazed at the activity surrounding them as they bought Po Boy Shrimp Sandwiches and took the time to enjoy the scenery. They toured the Museum of Flight and read the history of each plane that was obviously no comparison to today's engines, and both of them wondered how planes in those days were able to get off of the runway, let alone reach altitudes of 14,000 feet.

Although the weather was rainy, typically nine months out of every year in Seattle, they were having a great time exploring the city. The highlight of the trip for Doug was their visit to the Space Needle. He loved the 360-degree views of the bay from 600 feet above the water. The sight of the beautiful snow-capped Mount Rainier, the mighty Cascades, and the freezing Bay was breathtaking from the rotating Sky City Restaurant. Doug enjoyed the city immensely and could now mark this trip off of his bucket list. He would remember the nights even more than the days because of the special time he spent with Sydney.

On the plane trip home, Doug and Sydney discussed the plans to begin his production of prototype PDOB5 and he couldn't believe they had already worked on four projects together. He had met all critical specifications on time and under budget. With each contract completed, she presented Doug with a percentage of the commission, and each check had increased in its percentage of the total contract. Doug had earned more in the past year working with Sydney than collectively in his entire career. His skills had developed and his understanding of the industry had multiplied. He owed Sydney all the credit for bringing him this far, and he looked forward to so much more he could learn from her and her designs.

— CHAPTER 13 —

In October, one year after they had met, Sydney planned a trip for them to New York City. She knew that Doug had always wanted to visit and tour the Big Apple, and she was excited to surprise him. She told him about their trip as though it would be a normal business trip. Although she was vague in her answers to his questions about the new company and type of engine he would need to build, Doug did not find it unusual when Syd became very focused in her zone during the research of company projects. Doug packed more clothes than normal, taking a suit as well as a tux for a black-tie event Sydney said they would be attending. In the months since beginning his position at SCJ Enterprises, Doug had purchased better clothes and more shoes. He had never had a need for sneakers, hiking boots, dress shoes, and casual shoes. But Sydney jogged early each morning and had convinced Doug that he should join her on her laps around the river park. She had also introduced him to hiking trails in the beautiful mountains nearby, and he had to admit he felt better after several months of exercising. Doug actually liked getting outside after working in the garage hours on end.

Doug was excited about their upcoming trip; maybe more than any of their trips they had taken. When they were away from the garage, Sydney was a different person. Of course, during the presentations, she was stone cold, but once the contract was sealed, she let go and had fun. Their relationship was solid and steady, but sometimes he wondered if he would ever really break through to Sydney's heart. Although Doug maintained the apartment she provided for him, most of his nights were spent with Syd in her upstairs loft. He loved her so much, and although she had never told him that she loved him, he knew she did. Sydney always responded to his touch and met his passion with her own, often introducing new adult toys for them to try. Their lovemaking had reached stellar heights, and they had explored areas that he once thought would be taboo, but he thoroughly enjoyed each new adventure.

Soon after removing their seat belts on the flight to New York, Sydney excused herself to the restroom and stayed longer than Doug thought normal. He wondered if she was sick, and he should check on her. Just then his cell phone indicated that he had a text from Sydney asking him to come to the bathroom in the back of the plane. He knocked on the bathroom door expecting to see Sydney sick or upset only to have her pull him inside and kiss him passionately. She asked him if he would like to be a member of the five-mile-high club, and although he was concerned about another passenger knocking on the door, his body responded with a vengeance.

Sydney hopped up on the sink and wrapped her legs around his waist and hungrily forced his mouth open with her kisses. She had such a desire for him that she could hardly wait for him to remove her pants. As he stood in front of her and drove himself home, she held tightly onto the handicapped bars on either side of the sink. Her top was raised above her breasts, and he found his face nestled between them, sending her over the edge with excitement. Over and over, he pushed until she exploded into a cosmic orgasm, and her eyes rolled back in her head. Just as he kissed her gently pulling her bottom lip down with his teeth and explored the inside of her soft lip, the door wiggled, and someone knocked to come in.

"Just a second please," Sydney responded, laughing. "I will be out in just a minute."

As they scrambled, pulling their clothes back on, Doug straightened his hair and slicked her long auburn strands down a bit. They squeezed out of the plane's narrow door, and the waiting passenger grinned and of course knew what the two had been up to. Walking up the aisle to their seats, Sydney felt like all eyes were on them, and as soon as they took their seats, they buried their heads together giggling like teenagers.

"Oh my God, that was great, Syd!" said Doug, winded.

"What on Earth do you mean, Mr. O'Brien?" asked Sydney, feigning innocence and complete guilt at the same time. "Don't you always have sex on a plane?" she asked shyly.

"I thought that was the name of a drink, and to be honest, you know this already, I have only been on a plane seven times now, and each time has been with you. So, yes, Ms. James, I was an air virgin...until a few moments ago." Doug held her hand in his and kissed her knuckles one at a time. "I love you Sydney James, please love me too." Doug pleaded.

"Well, if I never teach you anything else in your career, we can proudly boast that you are now experienced in five-mile-high sexual activity, and by the way, It's Sex on the Beach, not Sex on a Plane that is a drink, " Syd responded as she laughed at his innocence.

"I will be sure to list that in the skills section on my updated resume," Doug replied smugly. "And for the record, I am a beer guy, not some fruity drink kind of guy."

Sydney laid her head on Doug's shoulder and slept during the remainder of the flight. He could not understand all the feelings he had for her. He knew that he loved her, and he was certain that she loved him too, but he needed more. Doug didn't have a strong desire to marry nor have children. He was happy in his new life with Syd, but even after making love and feeling completely satisfied, there was always a longing. What was it? Why did he feel this way? Doug wanted her to adore him as he did her. He wanted Sydney to want him as no one else, but didn't this tryst in the plane bathroom prove that she wanted him desperately? Syd had opened up in ways he never thought possible. Could their relationship be any better? Surely it would only get better and better.

— CHAPTER 14 —

As their plane landed at LaGuardia, Doug was not as impressed as he was when he saw the Hartsfield Atlanta Airport. There were as many travelers walking twice as fast, but the layout and design was not as sophisticated, which surprised Doug since he thought New York would be bigger and better in everything and every space. Passengers bumped into him without apologizing and retrieving their luggage was almost impossible. It took half an hour waiting to hail a cab, and finally, Sydney called for an Uber. They were booked in a suite at the Ritz Plaza in Manhattan, and the building looked taller than any he had ever seen. Even pictures and movies didn't give justice to the streets and activity in New York City. He had never seen so many people in such a small area, and they were all heading somewhere really quickly. It was like an ant farm with scrambling tiny little ants trying to rush from one site to the next.

Once in their thirtieth-floor suite, Doug opened the doors to the balcony and could see the thousands of tourists and residents zipping along on the streets below buying from street vendors, families eating in Central Park, and workers crammed onto both sides of the streets. It looked like a wave of people being rushed in like waves in the ocean with no control of where they'd land. But somehow, everyone seemed to arrive at their destinations. He had never seen so many people. It was only 4:00 in the afternoon yet was nearing dark on the streets because the sunlight could not penetrate through the tall skyscrapers that were built in such close proximity.

"So, what is our meeting agenda for this trip?" Doug asked Syd as she hung her clothes in the closet.

"We have no meeting agenda," she replied nonchalantly. "This trip is for you, for us. We met almost a year ago and have worked so hard. We have put in at least 60 hours each week with little or no downtime for relaxing. You have spent no time with your family and not complained one single time. You have dedicated yourself to your projects completely. You have remained focused on each prototype. Your engine productions have resulted in more contracts, and I could not have asked for a more dedicated employee. This has been the company's best financial year. This trip is for you. I know you have always wanted to visit New York, and this is your gift from me. I want to thank you for all your hard work," Sydney said.

"I don't know what to say, Syd, except thank you. There is nothing more that I want than to spend time with you. I love working with you, and I love our time together, and you owe me nothing more than what you give. You provide a great salary, an enormous benefits package, and an even better package at home. The commissions you have poured out this past year have provided money for my parents, my sister, and my nieces. I could have never helped them without this job. My dad now has a secure nest egg to fall back on if cancer strikes again, and a load has been lifted from them financially. My sis can now send her girls to a private school if she chooses or put that money into savings accounts for college. This has been the best year of my life. I can't believe you would do this for me."

Doug was obviously humbled by her thoughtfulness.

"There is no way we can make a dent in all the sights in this city, but I'd sure like to try. Maybe we can make this an annual event in October for us. One more thing I'd like to give you is your annual bonus that was outlined in your original employee contract," Sydney reached into her suitcase and handed him an envelope.

Doug opened it and inside was a check for one million dollars and his mouth fell open.

"What the hell is this for? I can't take this, Sydney. Are you trying to buy my contract out? Are you firing me? Will I have a job when we get back? Do you think you're my sugar mama?" As Doug turned to look at her, he seemed confused and almost angry.

"No, no of course not," Sydney seemed stunned that he would feel this way. "SCJ received a third quarter bonus five times that amount, and you deserve this for the work you produced on all the projects and especially with the Camden Engine. Please know that you earned every dollar, it is not a gift," Sydney explained.

She walked away and left him standing to stare at her as she went to run a shower and get the airport grime off her before they dressed for dinner. The hot, steamy water fogged the mirrors and condensation ran down onto sink. As Sydney closed her eyes and leaned back on the seat inside the shower the door opened, and Doug stepped in with her.

"I'm sorry if I seemed ungrateful. I just don't want to feel like you are keeping me. I love you, Sydney, and I want you to love me the same. Not as an employee or a boyfriend or even just a lover. I want all of you, every secret and hidden space inside you; I want you to belong to me. I want you to need me like I need you."

As he took her hair in his hands and twirled it around his fingers, he pulled her face up to meet his and started kissing her eyelids, her nose, her cheeks, and ever so gently running his tongue softly across her mouth. Syd didn't open her mouth to his but let his kisses run along her top lip and down to her neck. Her earlobes were so soft, and he whispered over and over that he loved her. With his left hand, Doug grasped both her wrists and placed them above her head, not allowing her to move. He was much stronger, and although Sydney struggled a bit, she loved every moment of the bondage. With his right hand, he found her sweet spaces, reaching the tiny spot that made her writhe with delight. He had a way to create pleasure every place he touched her body. He bit and nibbled hidden areas, creating just enough pain to make her squeal.

While Sydney was enjoying intense pleasure, Doug knelt on his knees before her and began kissing her stomach. She responded to his every move and found ecstasy like never before. Afterward, they soaped each other with the hotel's luxurious body wash, and Sydney shampooed his hair and face creating suds so thick he looked like Santa. As Syd washed the suds from his face and neck, she couldn't resist lathering up his lower body and rinsing it only to find him ready for her again. They both declared it would be hard to find the strength to dress for dinner and considered ordering room service.

The Empire State Building, the Statue of Liberty, and the new Freedom Towers were visible from their balcony, and they ate dinner late into the night drinking champagne and eating chocolate covered strawberries.

"I'd love to take you to the Smithsonian Institute and a play on Broadway while we are here. New York is a city where there is always so many exciting things to do," Sydney said. Doug was willing to go anywhere as long as he was with Sydney.

The next day was packed with activity, and Doug took photos of all of the attractions, so he could text them to his parents. Although they had never travelled north, his mom would enjoy all of the photos Doug was sharing with her.

Bert and Karen knew that Doug loved his new job, they knew he was enjoying the travel it included, and they suspected that he was in love with his boss as well. They had no idea how much he adored her and wanted to marry her. Sydney was not only his boss; she was his world. On the twenty-first floor of the Empire State Building, they walked to all four sides to view every possible angle of the city. It was astonishing how businesses could be built one after another on such tiny land lots. Prime real estate in New York City was far beyond the national average and only the wealthy could afford to live in the city. Few New Yorkers owned cars and rode in taxis or used Ubers for everyday travel. Doug could not fathom living this type of life as much as he loved his vehicles.

In the afternoon, they ferried to the Statue of Liberty as the wind whipped round causing them to snuggle in the cold, and Doug and Sydney dug their hands into their pockets to stay warm, kissing like teenagers for the entire ride. There were tears stinging Doug's eyes as he walked close to the Statue and felt his American pride. He couldn't imagine how early settlers felt as they saw the statue for the first time coming into the harbor. At the Freedom Towers Sydney found the name of a friend that died in the South Tower during the 911 attack. There were slips of paper and pencils provided to place over the name and scratch over it with a pencil like when they were in elementary school. The 911 memory museum held displays of firefighter hats, fire gear, wedding rings, and work radios left behind from rescue workers who had died in the attack. He could hardly breathe, thinking of the families' pain as they realized their heroes would never be coming home again. It brought back to memory that day of chaotic destruction, and they both stood in silence as they watched the video and tears slid down their cheeks.

They walked down Wall Street and saw the New York Times Building as well as Times Square. Doug bought gifts from FAO Schwarz for both of his nieces and knew they would be very excited. When Sydney saw the teal blue windows at Tiffany's, she strolled inside the store looking for nothing in particular. Doug told her he would like to purchase something for his mother and sister since neither would probably come to New York for a visit. He chose a signature Tiffany bracelet for his sister and a silver necklace with a K charm for his mother. Doug knew they would love the signature blue boxes as much as the gift inside. As Sydney was looking down the cases, Doug saw a gorgeous pair of small diamond loops he wanted to buy for Syd. They would match the tiny chain she always wore on her neck that her dad had given her so many years ago. He knew she would look spectacular in them. If he thought she would say yes, Doug would buy her a diamond engagement ring, but he knew that was too much to ask...

Maybe someday.

Later that evening, after watching the *Lion King* on Broadway, they walked blocks in the night air to their hotel laden with their purchases. Doug was starving and could not wait to feast at The Plaza Restaurant, which was rated five stars, and he had read reviews that it earned every delicious star.

The lobster and steak was succulent, and the roasted potatoes with carrots were grilled in a tangy sweet sauce. New Yorkers did not drink sweet tea, and Doug found it funny, but he didn't have a taste for wine, so he settled for water with lemon. His father would laugh when he heard that Doug didn't order a beer. He would accuse him of becoming uppity. After their meal, they went upstairs and slid into their pajamas and laid in bed watching Jimmy Kimmel until they fell asleep with Doug's arms wrapped around Sydney as she purred gently in her sleep. Doug couldn't image a more perfect day.

The week sped by as they enjoyed The Museum of Modern Art, rode the subway several times just to people watch, and picnicked in Central Park, joining in with the city residents who lived such a crazy exciting life. Children rode to school on the subways instead of buses without their parents, and no one said please and thank you. They weren't rude, just preoccupied. Life in the north was certainly different from the south in so many ways. Doug loved the city but would never want to live here.

They made love every morning before beginning their day of sightseeing and exploration and were sad to see the week come to an end. He felt like a little child excited to take souvenirs home to his family who had never traveled north of Kentucky. He couldn't wait to share his adventures with them. His mom would love seeing his photos of places she would probably never see, and his dad would love hearing all about the exhibits he had seen in the Smithsonian. Doug could not think his life could get better.

— CHAPTER 15 —

After their amazing NYC trip, life settled back into a routine for Sydney and Doug. Their work doubled in November and December with two new projects. One project was particularly difficult for Doug because he had never tinkered with an engine for a toy. However, the largest toy plane manufacturer had signed with SCJ Enterprises to develop a miniature engine they could house in an oversized drone airplane that would cost the consumer $10,000. This toy would not be suitable for young children, but for men who loved high tech toys, it would be worth the expense. Syd explained to Doug that he would not actually touch the parts or try to fit his large hands inside the engine but instead it would all be produced on screen with laser precision adaptation, and the prototype would be constructed robotically with microscopic arms that could reach into the inner chambers of the tiny engine housing. He was nervous but excited to explore this new way of production. Doug could only imagine what heights Sydney would push this production for the company.

On a Friday evening, as Sydney was driving home from a dinner with her uncle Joe, she received a text from Doug stating, "Syd, my dad's had a heart attack, I'm at the hospital, and I'll check in with you later, love you so much."

She quickly texted back to ask where Mr. O'Brian was being transported. She wanted to be there for Doug and knew he would be so worried until his father's prognosis was given. She didn't have to wait long for his response as her phone buzzed.

"Hi Doug, how's your dad?" Syd asked immediately.

"He didn't make it Syd. They did all they could, but he didn't pull through. The doctor said he had what's called a widow maker. It was massive and quick. Apparently he didn't respond to CPR during the ambulance trip or in the emergency room."

Doug was silent and for a moment Sydney was shocked beyond words. She had never even met the man that Doug loved and respected so much. Now it was too late.

"Where are you? I'll be right there." All she wanted to do was wrap her arms around him and comfort his hurting heart.

"No please don't come, I need this time with my family. They need me. I can't even wrap my head around this right now. It happened so fast. One minute, I'm working on my computer, and the next my father is dead. It doesn't seem real. I don't know what to say or do. My mother is devastated and completely silent, and my sister is beyond consoling, crying uncontrollably. I can't help them, and I feel helpless. They've never needed me before; they always had Dad. He took care of them and made our family feel safe, and now he's gone. How will they make it without him?" Doug sounded distraught.

"Please let me come to you. You need someone too. You can't shoulder this alone."

"No, I just need to be with them right now. I will call you later," he said as he disconnected before Syd could respond.

She thought about calling around to the hospitals in the area. There were only a few that a cardiac patient would be taken in an emergency. But Sydney decided to give Doug the time he needed with his family. They had not crossed this type of hurdle in their professional or personal relationship yet. In the past year and a half together, they had fought, slammed doors, cursed, cried, loved, apologized, and Doug had even cared for her during a horrible strand of the flu. He had held her head during vomiting and rubbed her aching limbs until he fell asleep beside her, but not death. Doug had listened many times of how hurt Sydney was when her father died. He had been her sounding block when she questioned if she had provided the best for her mother after her father's death. For the first time, Sydney realized her overwhelming love for Doug and wanted to be there for him as he had been for her for the past year. But everyone had their own way of dealing with tragedy, and Sydney always respected other's feelings. This time would be no different. Doug needed time alone with Karen and Becca, and she would give it to him. When he needed her, she would be there ready to help in any way he would allow.

Doug did not come to the garage the next day but texted Syd several times letting her know that he was home with his mom helping her make funeral arrangements. His dad had been a simple man, and they would have a simple service for him. He gave Sydney the arrangements and told her that he was staying at his parents' home to be close to his mom and sister. Syd ordered an enormous arrangement of peace lilies and peonies from the company addressed to his family and called her caterer to order a variety of foods to be delivered to the funeral home for his family. Sydney worked late into the night and couldn't sleep, thinking of the heartbreaking pain she knew he was experiencing.

Around 2:00 in the morning, Syd heard the apartment door opening and knew Doug was home. Her heart ached for him, and she ran to meet him in the living room to wrap her arms around him. She had preset the coffee maker earlier as well as stocking the fridge with cold beer because she didn't know if he would want to drink and talk or drink and sleep or just drink and drink. He remained silent as she wrapped her arms around his waist as he dug his large hands in her hair and pulled her head to his chest as tears dripped onto her head from his cheeks.

As Doug sat on the couch he stared at the floor. Sydney saw the deep circles under his beautiful eyes, and his dark curls had not seen a brush in days. She climbed on his lap facing him and laid her head on his shoulder hugging him close. He had still not said a word but seemed to relax a bit under her embrace.

"He's gone, Syd. I cannot believe I don't have a father anymore. It is beyond the worst pain I have ever felt in my life. I don't even know how to express the crush I feel in my chest." Doug held onto her like a child needed his mother.

"You don't have to say anything, Doug. You don't have to try to explain. These are times that I think God knows our aching heart and will provide the peace you will need for the coming days ahead."

As they sat for almost an hour in the dim light, he began to respond to her presence and looked up into her face with those brilliant blue eyes and asked, "Will you make love to me, Syd? I need to be with you now."

Without waiting for her response, he picked her up in his big arms and took her to their bed. Sydney unbuttoned his crumpled shirt and rolled Doug over onto his stomach as she sat over him and began massaging his shoulders and back. She rolled him over on his back and began kissing his face and neck. He was so tense from two days of being strong for his family and providing a shoulder on which everyone could rely. She kneaded his arms and thighs with the palms of her hands down to his waist and as she removed her pajama top she laid over him as he began to stroke her hair.

Lying on top of his massive frame, Sydney wanted Doug to know that he was loved and secure. She whispered that she loved him over and over giving him the reassurance he needed during his time of grief. Syd had never told Doug her feelings but wanted him to know how much he meant to her. She gently slid her tongue over his ears whispering how he made her feel and telling him how much she needed him in her life. She slid the jeans off his waist and her hands deeply massaged his lower legs then upward finding special areas that she knew drove him crazy.

As she kissed down his stomach, she slid her mouth down until she found her own pleasure. Doug sat up to face her and watched her as she made love to him. He manipulated her hips at the pace he needed, and Sydney found his rhythm as he reached behind her to caress her back. As always, his eyes never left her face, and she watched the tension drain from him and knew she was easing his pain along with giving him pleasure. It was as though he couldn't love her enough as over and over again, their climax was met in a different position and a stronger intensity than the previous one. He cried himself to sleep afterward as Sydney held him tightly.

Doug dreaded the next day with all his heart because he had never experienced death before. He wanted to be by his mother's side and to comfort his younger sister, but he needed Sydney beside him for strength.

As they arrived at the funeral home, Syd realized she would be meeting Doug's family and friends for the first time. They had been together for 18 months, and he had never introduced her to his family. She had never met his father before he died and was sorry that she missed the opportunity. They rarely discussed his family except in light conversation and realized she knew very little about them. This was a man she was in love with and wanted to share his life but did not know the most important people that meant the most to him. Sydney felt ashamed that she had never asked to be a part of their lives as well. This was not the best time to be introduced to family and be expected to carry on conversations as though it was any normal day. Syd realized she was nervous, and her hands were sweating as they entered the funeral home.

As Syd and Doug arrived in her BMW, she realized this was going to be a very simple affair. There were old trucks, older cars and even older motorcycles in the parking lot. Of all people, Syd loved cars of all kinds, but she did not want to be judged because she drove an import. She wore a simple black Vera Wang pantsuit with a triple strand of rare ivory Panama pearls on her neck, ears, and wrists. Her black heels and matching Marc Jacobs clutch, which she intended to be simple, created a sleek, polished and high-end appearance that she didn't really want to give. Sydney was always poised and elegant, but it was never her intention to be haughty, especially around Doug's family and friends. She wanted them to know she loved him and that she was a perfect match for him.

Sydney was first introduced to his mother and sister, and she felt that she was being inspected and not sure that she scored highly on their report card. There were so many names to remember and connections to make that she began to feel overwhelmed in this world of Doug's where she was not a member. Syd found a seat in a corner where she could sit out of the way and allow Doug space to receive visitors and condolences. A slide show played hundreds of photos of Doug as a child with his dad playing with dogs, he and his sister playing chase, photos of pets, horses, and of course, his mom and dad in happier times. His childhood looked so fun and full of wonderful memories. She felt such sadness for him that his childhood was now over, and he would forever miss his father.

Sydney was concentrating on the power point when she heard a man's laughter as he said, "Yeah, Doug's all uppity since he found him a sugar mama, and he ain't got time for his buddies no more."

Another male voice chimed in, "Did you see what he drove up in? I always knew he liked cars, but damn, now that's a nice ride. It's probably hers, and he's her driver."

They all laughed as they mocked Doug's new lifestyle.

"Well, she's a beaut," said another.

"The car or the chick?" said the first to comment.

"Both...they must both have a hell of an engine under their hood. Ol' Doug's always been a lady's man. He's just got one with money now, and he ain't lookin' for greener pastures. You see his mama's Facebook page? She posted pictures he sent her from Washington, California, New York City, Dallas, Chicago, and he had never even been on a plane 'for he met her. Now he's buildin' the damn things. Heard she put him up in a penthouse, gave him a car, and pays him a million a year just to keep her little engine all greased up."

They all laughed again, and she felt nauseated.

Sydney wandered around the funeral home giving Doug distance, and it seemed that everywhere she went someone was discussing Doug's "new wealth" or his "sugar mama" and once she overheard someone say he now had an "old lady." It made Sydney mad that these people who he referred to as his friends had no idea as to his talent or contribution to the engineering industry. She wanted to stand on the casket and scream out that he was brilliant in the engine production field and that because of his hard work millions of dollars had been poured into providing jobs all across the nation. His engines were in planes that carried donor hearts and kidneys to critical patients awaiting transplants from Seattle to Key West, Florida, and hundreds of hospitals in between. He had built a prototype that was donated to the Wings of Hope Foundation. The foundation provided free transportation for underprivileged children with special needs who desperately needed to fly to hospitals for treatment. Every twin engine plane was owned by the WOH Corporation, donating trips to these families and never charged a fee... and Doug developed them. His hands alone had worked 60- and 80-hour work weeks without resting, only to fly to meetings across the country to meet with sponsors who contributed funds to many cancer centers, and on this very day aerospace engineers were waiting for his productions to roll off the belt to send to NASA for future flight explorations. No, they didn't know this Doug at all.

Sydney had heard enough, and she needed to get some air. She gently tapped Doug on the shoulder and asked him for her car keys. He gave them to her but asked her to ride with him in the family car to the cemetery. Syd just lowered her head and shook her head no. She told him that she would meet him later and that he was needed to stay by his sister and mother. Doug looked confused, but he heard his name called by another friend and turned away to answer. When he turned back to look for Syd, she was gone. As she walked down the hallway to the front door, she looked up into the eyes of a young woman that Syd knew immediately was someone from Doug's past. She looked like someone that Doug would like. Her hair was coal black and cut into a sleek bob that framed her beautiful face, and she was petite, maybe even smaller than Sydney. Their eyes met and Sydney smiled as she walked past her.

Once past her, the young woman said, "You won't keep him. He is not the keeping kind."

Sydney straightened to her full height and said, "Excuse me? Are you speaking to me?"

The pretty young lady revealed to her, "I am Jennifer, Doug's ex, and he won't stay with you. All of your money and fancy cars will entertain him for a while, but he is not the keeping kind. He will tire of you and this sweet new life of his, and believe me; he will come back to the country to his roots. He may already be tired of you. Have you not noticed that he is not working on Tuesday and Thursday evenings? Well, he has been with me on those nights, and our pillow talk keeps me updated on all your attempts to keep him.

"But it's not working. He will leave, and when he does, I am here waiting. So, go ahead and buy him cars, apartments, clothes, and make him a rich man. He will still turn on you in the end, just like he did me the first time around," she said smugly. "But this time it will be different. He will come home to stay...right where he belongs."

Sydney felt the vomit rising in her throat and knew that any moment she would cover the pretty young lady's blouse in the vilest explosion.

"Well, Jennifer, it was nice to meet you," Syd managed to reply, "and I am not sure what Doug has told you, but he is my employee and as long as he doesn't divulge the secrets to our engine prototypes, I could care less what your pillow talk consists of. If he shares those secrets, he will be slapped with a multibillion-dollar lawsuit, so hopefully your talk is all on a personal level, or he will come to you as poor as a church mouse," Sydney told her as she walked past her.

Syd could not walk to her car fast enough, and as she slid into the creamy leather seats, tears dripped onto her lap. How could she allow herself to be manipulated like this? She thought she was smarter than the average female. She let her guard down, and damn it if she didn't go and fall in love. Well, not this time. Sydney would go to the cemetery to support Doug and then she would be on her way home.

As she slid her car into a space far in the back of the funeral procession, Syd hoped that she could slip in unnoticed and then leave while Doug was busy caring for his mother and sister. But as soon as she walked up the hill to the plot, he patted an empty seat beside his for her, and she quietly shook her head no. The service began and was short and sincere with the pastor quickly concluding in prayer. There were country neighbors, cowboys, and family members all dressed casually, and Sydney was struck by how she stood out among them. It was not her intension to be noticed, but she was different, and it was obvious. In their profession, she and Doug were more the same. They lived each day with their heads buried in computers and inside the mechanics of an engine; however, in the outside world they were far more different. Syd had not realized just how different until Jennifer and all of Doug's buddies made it perfectly clear. She had been such a fool and was just now realizing it.

Without looking back Sydney drove home to the garage and ran up the stairs to her sanctuary. Here, she could shut out the world, but the thoughts were swirling in her head and causing rage to boil inside her.

— CHAPTER 16 —

Doug did not come in that night, and Sydney was glad that he chose to stay with his family or Jennifer or wherever he was as long as it was not with her. She didn't see him the next day but several times heard him working downstairs, but she did not want to face him, not yet. Probably by now his girlfriend had filled him in on their brief meeting, and he was trying to find a way to let her down gently. She didn't need his pity or to be let down gently. She was a much stronger woman than he had ever seen. After lunch, Syd strolled down in her cut off jean shorts and her socked feet. Her hair was pulled back in a ponytail and her glasses were sitting on top of her head.

"Good afternoon, Doug, how are you doing? Do you have time to go over the stats from the PDOB10?" Sydney asked casually.

Doug walked over to pull her into his arms only to have her pull away and glare at him.

"Syd, what's wrong with you? I really needed you yesterday. I'm upset with you because I know how you hate funerals, but I really could have used your support at the cemetery. I would have loved for you to get to know my family at my mom's home so that they could also get to know you better. I wanted you to see the house I had built for my mom; she loves it and would have loved to thank you for the opportunities you have given me. Hell, Syd, I just needed you, was that too much to ask?" Doug was obviously hurt that she hadn't been there for him.

"Doug, we need to talk about something. I wanted to wait, but since you brought it up, we might as well discuss it now," Sydney took a few steps back and sat on his bar stool.

"Okay... Something wrong?" he looked sincere, but he didn't fool her; not anymore.

"I don't think our partnership will work any longer. I have spoken to my attorneys, and we have a prepared a severance package that should be satisfactory. You don't even have to work out a two week's notice. You are welcome to use the apartment until the end of the month and then you can give me the keys once your things are packed. Of course, I will buy your part of the prototypes at the projected value. If you would like to keep one of the cars you prefer to drive, please take one for yourself." Sydney was stone-face as she explained the procedure. Doug paled as she talked and he felt a nausea wave hit him in the gut.

"Syd, what on earth?" he asked. "What did I do wrong? Did I screw up an engine? I will fix whatever it is. How can you just fire me and not try to work out the kinks? We have been working together two years, and you haven't even had one complaint that we couldn't correct. We are the best team there is, you can't just throw this away! And what about us? I want to spend my life with you. Hell, you are my life."

He was obviously distraught as he was pacing the office. Doug couldn't imagine what could be so wrong that they could not work it out. Sure, he had made mistakes in his designs, but they had always worked endlessly until the errors were corrected. How could she just give up on their designs? How could she do it without him? How could he live without her? He couldn't imagine not being with her every single day. His chest was pounding and his heart was racing. This was his life now, and he could not even begin to think about one minute without her in it. He stopped pacing and just stared at her shamelessly with tears pouring down his face.

"Doug, you are an asshole, and I want no part of you any longer. I heard enough from your friends at the funeral home, and what they didn't say, Jennifer did. I was embarrassed; no, I was mortified at the things said by your friends. But then to have your girlfriend confront me in the lobby and tell me all the little nighttime secrets you have been sharing with her. Thank you for confiding our 'private life' to her," Sydney said as she closed her fingers in quotation marks. "God, Doug, you disgust me! The sad part is that on Tuesdays and Thursdays, I thought you needed space, maybe some time alone since we worked and lived together. I thought you might be going out for a beer with the guys. I had no idea you were going to see Jennifer and then coming home to me. You didn't even have the decency to shower before having sex with me after you had been with her. I will never be referred to again as someone's hot mama or sugar mama. I can't believe I fell for you, your eyes, your hair, your body—and I let myself fall completely in love with you.

"I ignored every single warning my dad taught me. He always cautioned me about getting involved with coworkers and especially employees. I was so stupid. I should have listened. Jennifer told me how your pillow talk revealed our private conversations and how tired you have become of this lifestyle. Well, let me tell you one thing: if you have broken our confidentiality agreement, you will not be able to afford as much as a beat up station wagon. I will sue your pants off and laugh while walking out of the courthouse. Now I am going upstairs, and DO NOT follow me. I want your office cleaned out, and I want you gone by the weekend."

— CHAPTER 17 —

Before Sydney could reach the stairs, Doug had his hand on her upper arm and turned her around to face him.

"No, we cannot end like this. You have to listen to me. I have not been unfaithful to you. Those guys are idiots and just stupid rednecks. They are jealous because I have such a great life with you. Even without the money, I'd have a great life with you. Look at you, Syd, you are so much more than I deserve. You shouldn't have given me the time of day. I am just a shade tree mechanic that you accidently met, and I never stop wondering why you gave me a chance in your company much less allowed me to love you. You are every breath that I take each day. I have never told anyone that you are my hot mama or sugar mama. I would not disrespect you that way. I have never discussed money with anyone, not even my family. They have no idea how much you pay me. They only know that I have given them more in the last two years than ever in my life.

"And Jennifer, don't even get me started on her. She is a liar. She cheated on me with my best friend, who was also married at the time. She broke up with me to be with Steve and broke up his marriage to Laura. I left home to make a better life for myself in Atlanta. She had an affair on Steve and broke up that marriage, only to leave him for some other gloat. You can't believe one word she ever says. I have only seen her twice since we broke up five years ago, and that was too soon for me," Doug talked so fast and was so angry his face was turning red.

"There is no way she lied about the things she said you told her. How on Earth would she know about your apartment, your cars, and your clothes? How would she know you left here every Tuesday and Thursday nights? I will not fall for your lies again. I am smarter than that, and we are finished here," Syd was screaming as she started up the stairs two at a time. "You get one shot with me, and you had your shot...and missed."

Doug's voice softened as he gently said her name.

"Syd, can I just tell you one thing?"

She turned and looked at his bright blue eyes and her heart ached for him.

"I have been going to night classes for the past nine months. Every Tuesday and Thursday night, I have engineering and statistics classes. I know I will never be as smart as you, Syd, and Harvard will never be in my cards, but if I could finish my degree, I thought I might deserve you just a little more. I wanted to keep it a secret until I finish my credits. I thought you would be proud of me, and we could stand on more of an equal ground. Phillip, who is an old friend of mine from high school, is taking some of the same classes with me. We met at a bar last year and started talking about how we both needed to finish what we started in college. One thing led to another, and we ended up registering for the same classes, and here we are. The only way I can figure Jennifer would know these things is from Phil. A few weeks ago, I gave a presentation when this semester first began. Please let me show you what I am talking about."

Doug walked over to his computer and brought the screen up to show Sydney the paper he had written for the class assignment.

"Please read this, and you will see what I read to the class."

Doug moved aside so that she could sit down and read the document. Sydney began to read the beautifully written article where Doug explained his childhood and how his family could not afford even their basic everyday needs. She went on to read how he had always wanted more and desired to go to college. He wrote of the chance she had given him without an engineering degree and how they are making their mark in the engineering world as a team. She read the reasons he wanted to earn a degree and the opportunities he had been presented in this position. The cars, the financial success, and even his new way of thinking about success were evident in his writings.

Syd sat spellbound reading the sincerely in his paper. He didn't mention that he was in love with his employer, but his admiration for her was obvious in his writing. He explained that he had to read it to the entire class, and Phillip was in this class. He knew that Jennifer and Phillip were still friends, but he didn't know that he was that close to her. It didn't surprise him the lengths Jennifer would go to destroy anyone who achieved even the slightest bit of success if it did not involve her.

"He must have told Jennifer about it. We have known each other since high school. It is just my luck that they are still friends and talk often. I swear, I have not seen her. She is a vindictive bitch, and I hate her. She never wanted me to have more while we were together. She didn't want me to be successful. She wanted a little two-bedroom trailer on five acres somewhere with several children. That was not my dream, but I was willing to settle for what I thought I deserved. However, she couldn't seem to settle just for me. Her only other dream was to hook up with every other guy in the county. She always loved drama, and believe me, she created plenty...

"Sydney, what they said at the funeral home was terrible, but I would never leave you. I will never tire of you or of us. You are the one and only for me, and I don't want to live without you, ever."

Doug took her face in his hands, and his gaze melted her heart. He looked deep into her eyes, and she melted into his arms. She couldn't resist him. She believed him despite all the hurtful words she had heard from his friends. "I love you, Syd, more than life itself. I want to marry you, I want to have a family with you, and I never want to fight again. Not about this." Doug kissed her long and hard and held her like he could never let her go.

Doug stood behind her and pulled her arms around his neck as his hands found her smooth stomach and then moved up towards her neck. He ran his fingers underneath the waist of her pants and then moved down. She welcomed him as he unzipped her pants and slid them down. He pulled her legs up so that he could find her most sensitive spaces. His hands worked their magic, sending her to heights only he could make her climb.

Syd's cries of satisfaction became louder and more intense. Doug held her in a tight grip as he removed his clothes, and they made love like their world would end tomorrow, and they would never have this chance again. He spun Syd's body around and faced her, looking deep into her eyes, willing her to see through to the very core of his heart.

After making love again on his office couch, they lay spent and grateful for their intense love and once again hopeful for the future together. Sydney raked her fingers through his wet hair and the curls that framed his face. She had to believe him, she had to trust him; her heart gave no choice. He had won her soul, and there was no turning back. Sydney would risk everything in her life to hold on to this love they had found, and she would fight to keep it. They curled up on the soft leather sofa and slept deeply.

Her last memory was of him whispering how much he loved her over and over again.

— CHAPTER 18 —

As spring weather warmed the river front and the chilly winter winds ceased whipping around the city, Sydney found her business booming more than ever. She and Doug rarely saw each other during the work week. They emailed and texted updates constantly during the day and were so tired they fell asleep right after dinner each night.

One Friday afternoon in March, Syd received a call from Acme Canine Suppliers requesting she fly to Portland, Maine, to discuss an idea their management team was working on and wanted her advice. She couldn't imagine how her company could assist in the animal industry, but they thought a short trip north would be fun. Sydney booked a beautiful bed and breakfast inn for their trip that was rated among the most romantic on the east coast. She loved lighthouses and especially Portland Head in Maine. She was excited to take this trip with Doug.

It was still cold in the northeast, and a heavy parka was necessary to ward off the cold winds. The B&B was a large white five-bedroom Victorian with lace edging around the roof line. Built in the early 1900s, its massive winding staircase and ornate moldings had been carefully preserved and revealed little age. The room Syd reserved was on the third floor and displayed a large marble fireplace where a fire was crackling when they were shown where to put their luggage. The guests were enjoying wine, hot chocolate, and fresh warm scones in the upstairs dining room. Their furnishings were dark mahogany with intricate pale pink accessories. Flickering candles provided the perfect ambiance needed for a cold night and snuggling underneath the thick down covers.

The next morning, Sydney was glad she brought warm wool pants and a cashmere sweater to wear. The light dusting of snow made for slick walking, so her duck boots would keep her feet toasty as they strolled along the waterfront. When she and Doug arrived at the Acme Warehouse, they were surprised to see dogs everywhere. Normally animals were not allowed in a manufacturing facility due to work hazards and safety guidelines. Not only were dogs playing and resting in the plant and offices, but also on the streets of Portland. Every store and business welcomed dogs. Even restaurants had leash tie downs, water bowls, and cute dog houses where customers could latch their dog leash for comfort during their meal. Most businesses provided doggy biscuits or snacks for their furry friends. Portland was a friendly area, and apparently dog therapy played a large part in its success. It seemed to be a happy city and they both loved being there.

Frank Markell, ACME's owner, pitched his idea to Sydney, and she could see how much his love for dogs brought about interest in all things canine. He wanted Sydney to design a tiny mechanical device that could be planted inside a dog's skin to indicate his internal body temperature. She understood how extreme the temperatures became during the winter months, and Frank explained that each year hundreds of dogs were treated for frostbite on their paws from slight to severe. Some longhaired breeds died from their wet coats that quickly froze creating internal organ shut down. It was common to see dogs wearing all weather boots and jackets during the winter months, but many could not keep them on due to the bad fit and their internal temperature could drop very quickly, causing them to have seizures and, in many cases, quickly die. The device he wanted to produce would indicate the dog's internal temperature and alert the owner to take action immediately. Without an internal alarm, a dog's chance of survival would decrease due to the short window of time allowing the temperature to slowly warm at a safe speed. A sudden rise in the internal temperature could prove equally as damaging as a rapid drop. With the alert, the owner would have more time to bring the pet inside and receive the proper care. Thousands of dogs' lives could be saved each year, and he was asking Sydney to create the design to make that happen. Syd had always loved dogs and had many pets during her childhood. Her dad was always rescuing deserted animals that needed bandaging or just a meal and a bed. Her mother had complained many times about Syd and her dad bringing in every stray in the neighborhood. There had never been a dog she couldn't love, and she would always try to talk her dad into keeping them for her own...most of the time he said yes. Syd had a small terrier named Tootsie who been her sidekick for over five years but died when she wandered into the road and was hit by a speeding driver early one morning. After Tootsie passed away Sydney just didn't want to grow attached to another dog and hadn't owned one since. Sometimes she missed a furry bed buddy to snuggle beside, but with her travel schedule, there was no way she could be a responsible pet owner. Besides, now she had Doug to snuggle with, and he was bigger, not as furry, but he kept her very warm at night. If she agreed to design this product, it would be different than anything she had ever attempted before. The new venture would require smaller, more intricate technical details as well as clearing legal hurdles from animal rights laws to ensure the safety of the device. It would not do for one single dog to be injured by this product. One costly mistake could put her out of business if her device injured or killed an animal due to negligence. Syd would make sure that did not happen.

Later in the day, Frank took them to meet the local veterinarian, who gave a demonstration on the computer program his office used for heat detection in animals and explained how his team could detect the animal's temperature then slowly raise it to keep the dog safe and prevent frostbite on the limbs and pneumonia in the lungs. A large percentage of heat can be lost through the paws, and unfortunately, walking directly on icy roads and freezing floors can cause direct injury to the pads, heart, and lungs. Without paw shoes, heart failure can occur in a matter of minutes once the dog's feet make contact with an icy surface. If Sydney's alarm worked correctly and the pet owner followed the directions, no pup would ever have to suffer thermal injury and could lead a happy healthy life, even in the frigid temperatures of the northeast weather. Syd's mind immediately wandered to other areas that could benefit from this type of alert in dog safety, such as fire rescue, snow rescue, and other extreme temperature situations.

Sydney and Doug then toured the city humane society and looked at many dogs with cracked or infected paws and even some that were walking with amputated limbs due to frostbite. It broke her heart to see dogs of all sizes hobbling on three legs when they should be running and playing and leading more active lives had their feet not frozen. Syd sat in the puppy playroom, and Doug watched as she played like a kid at Christmas interacting with the dogs. She was a natural pet lover, and he had never seen this side of her. She giggled as the dogs licked her face, jumped all over her lap, and begged for her attention, which she freely gave. It didn't matter to her that she was wearing expensive clothes or that their little sharp nails picked at her beautiful sweater. To Sydney, she was back in her childhood playing with puppies on the farm with her daddy, and her days were carefree. Doug saw the little girl in her eyes, and he enjoyed watching her laugh and play. He knew she would agree to this project, without a doubt, he knew.

The next morning was bright and sunny and unseasonably warm, so they rented a car and drove up the coast to the Portland Head Lighthouse, where the wind blew cold and strong. The white lighthouse was not tall, but at the top they saw tiny boats in the distance that looked like pieces of candy floating on the ocean. There was a strong breeze, and Sydney wanted to rent a boat and go sailing for the day. After riding through town and admiring the old colonial and Cape Cod homes, Sydney told Doug she would like to buy a vacation home here one day. After eating fresh lobster and shrimp at a local port restaurant, Doug agreed he could spend a lot of time in this beautiful coastal town and started thinking about buying a home with Syd.

Back at the B&B, they packed a bag of extra clothes, a blanket, and asked the inn keeper to prepare a picnic basket for their outing. They walked down to the board walk holding hands to register for their boat rental. Sydney was wearing white capris with a light sweater and sneakers and had packed a heavy jacket in case the winds were cold on the water. The waves were white with their glistening caps and made it impossible to see without dark glasses. Sydney had sailed as a teen and young adult, but it had been years, and Doug had only been on the water once and not at all as an adult. Once his father took him on a deep-sea fishing trip, but Doug vomited the entire day and hated the smell of sea water after their day cruise.

After hoisting the sails, Doug caught on quickly to tying them off and opening them to full sail to catch the wind. He had never seen a more brilliant day, and Syd was so beautiful with her long auburn hair dancing in the whipping wind. The waves were more calm and sailing was easy on the smooth ocean once they left port. Since it was a weekday, there were only a few boats on the water and none near them. It was as if they were lone sailors crossing the Atlantic. After a while, they were hungry, so they dropped the sails to sit still and enjoy their picnic. Their hostess had prepared boiled shrimp, coleslaw, and hushpuppies for them as well as a thermos of clam chowder, which was still piping hot. She sent along a carafe of wine and an assortment of cheese, crackers, grapes, and strawberries.

After finishing their meal, both Syd and Doug were ready to lie in the afternoon sun for a nap. The sun's rays burned hot through their clothes, and Sydney decided to remove hers and enjoy their solitude in the buff. The ocean was endless, and they were all alone as far as they could see. Doug watched her adoringly as she shed her shoes, pants, and top. She lay on the deck in only her bra and panties without a care in the world. It didn't take but a few seconds for Doug to remove his clothes and lie beside her on the blanket. As the wine warmed them, Doug rolled over on his side and looked down at her flawless face as she closed her eyes and rested.

Doug traced his finger down the profile of her face, "I can't imagine a better day than today. I want to remember us like this forever. When we are old and gray, I want to look back on this day and think of how calm and peaceful our world was." Doug talked as though he was already reminiscing.

Sydney reached up and pulled him on top of her and kissed him hungrily. She longed for him every time she heard his voice, and when he told her how much he loved her she wanted him even more. Syd wrapped her legs around him as he removed her lacy panties and moaned as he pulled her hips up to match his in an even rhythm. Their lovemaking was tender and slow, then fierce and fast, repeating the same motions over and over until they were completely satisfied in the moment. She rolled over beside him and sat up as he looked at her in the afternoon sunlight. God, she was lovely, and she was his. He had never felt so alive in his life and he would remember this moment forever. They relaxed basking in the warm afternoon sun and fell asleep to the rocking of the sailboat.

After returning the boat to the harbor, Syd and Doug were tired from their day on the water. They had replaced their summer clothes with thick sweaters and wool caps. The amber sun was setting, and the wind picked up as the temperatures dropped. The B&B hostess lit a fire in each room in the evenings, creating a warm ambiance. The house smelled amazing, like hot vegetable soup and garlic bread. Doug realized he was starving and just wanted to curl up by the fireplace with a big bowl of something hot and filling. He and Syd changed into warm pajamas after a steaming shower together and curled up on the bed. They watched old reruns of the *I Love Lucy* show, and Sydney kept waking Doug from his slumber with her laughter at the antics of Lucy and her sidekick Ethel. Syd found each episode funnier than the previous one, and soon she found herself laughing uncontrollably. She fell asleep snuggling under the covers with the TV on. It was the end to a perfect week.

— CHAPTER 19 —

Four weeks after beginning the design of PDOB15-Canine, Sydney and Doug were ready to turn over their design to Frank. His team was anxious to take it to production and get it on the shelves for their customers. He wanted the devices fully approved and ready to market for the upcoming winter season. Work was ticking along smoothly, and they were busier than ever. One afternoon, one week before Sydney's birthday, Doug called upstairs to make sure she was in a good mood and not buried beneath papers in research.

"Hey, Syd are you busy, can I come up?" Doug always respected Sydney's privacy and never barged in on her work.

"Sure, come on up," she said as she realized it was late, and she had been working for hours without eating. She was hungry and hoped Doug was bringing dinner up with him.

When Doug came in, he was carrying a huge box wrapped in bright red birthday paper and a large bow on top. He was grinning from ear to ear, and she wondered what he had up his sleeve.

"What in the world?" she asked confused. It was a week until her birthday. What couldn't wait until then? In their three years together, Doug had turned Syd's disdain for surprises into anticipation like a child when he would bring her gifts. It was often that he surprised her with flowers, trinkets, books or movies. He loved watching her eyes twinkle and dance when he caught her off guard. She was like a little girl, and he loved to spoil her.

"I have a surprise for you, and I need to give it to you now," Doug said as he tried to keep the box balanced. Suddenly, the box and paper came alive as a curly blond puppy bounced out of the big box, barking and running over to greet Sydney.

"Oh my God, Doug, what have you done?" Sydney squealed with apparent delight. "I can't have a dog! Oh, you sweet thing, you are beautiful. Doug, I just can't have a dog. You know my schedule. She is so beautiful. Can I have a dog? Do I have time? Oh, I want her so much. Do you think I can keep her? What if I don't have time for her? What if I neglect her? What if she gets out in the road and gets killed... Oh I love her already!"

Syd was beside herself with delight. The more excited Syd became, the more the puppy jumped and down on her back legs.

"Calm down, everything will be fine. She is a Golden Doodle and will be a medium to large size curly mass of energy. She is crate and house trained, and I think you will be a great dog mom. It was so obvious how much you love dogs when we were in Maine, and I couldn't resist. Congratulations, you're a mommy! I can't think of anyone better to be her mom." Doug could see she would be spoiled, adored, and pampered by Sydney.

"Oh, Doug, how can I ever thank you! She is so precious, and I love her so much already." Sydney said with tears streaming down her cheeks. "What is her name?"

"What do you want it to be?" he asked as she looked closely into the pup's sweet face hoping to find the answer there. "How about Lucy?" Doug asked. "Because I've never seen you laugh as hard as when we were watching the old reruns of the *I Love Lucy* show in Maine, and that is where I witnessed your deep love for dogs. That's where I got the idea to get you a dog for your birthday."

"Lucy it is then. Lucy, do you like this name? Lucy James-O'Brian, you will be called, and I love you to pieces already."

That night, Lucy found her place in the bed between Sydney and Doug. Doug wondered what on Earth he was thinking, and would they ever sleep alone again? Lucy curled up under Syd's legs, and Doug watched as they both slept peacefully.

The next few weeks were hectic as Syd and Doug took turns taking Lucy out to house train her, but she was very smart and took to potty training quite well. Lucy became Sydney's shadow and went everywhere right by her side. She lay under Sydney's desk while she worked and slept like a sweet baby. Every afternoon, they took Lucy to the dog park by the river where she made puppy friends and learned to socialize. She whimpered when the veterinarian gave her immunizations, and Sydney cried as well. She pranced around their home in a sparkling pink collar with her name engraved on it. Syd had a microchip inserted and even had her nails painted. The amount of money spent on her dog bed, bowls, food, and toys was insane, but Sydney didn't care. She worked hard, didn't have children, and was happy to buy whatever she could to make Lucy's life perfect. This was her child now, and she was spoiling her rotten. Lucy had a bed in Doug's office, one in the production lab, a pink fluffy bed with her name on it in the upstairs bedroom and another by the couch in the living room. This dog knew she was loved. Often Syd would find her asleep on her back with all of her legs extended exposing her tummy to be rubbed by any passerby.

After several months, Sydney asked Doug how he felt about adding a second dog to be a playmate for Lucy, and even though a little hesitant, he could never say no to any request she made. They felt it would be better to get a pup about the same age and size as Lucy and hopefully they would bond. After shopping the Pet Finder website day after day, they finally adopted a male of the same breed, and he was deep chocolate with deep blue eyes. Doug named him Ricky and was happy to have some male testosterone in the house. Lucy and Ricky became fast friends and soon were terrorizing the garage. Ricky had his own toys but wanted every toy that Lucy wanted. He would place three or four tennis balls in his mouth and dared Lucy to take even one of them. They ran up and down the stairs and all around the warehouse until they would collapse in complete exhaustion. At night, the dogs would snuggle together on their big plush bed finally giving Doug and Sydney some much needed time alone in their king size human bed. James-O'Brian party of four...their family was complete.

— CHAPTER 20 —

After months of working with the ACME Canine project then adopting Lucy and Ricky, Sydney needed a break. She and Doug had been together almost five years and worked tirelessly. They had produced award winning engine designs and electrical prototypes. Their work had been recognized by the ASPCA for canine betterment, NASA aerospace engineering advancement for efficiency and environmental design production, as well as several other governing agencies. Sydney and Doug had traveled all across the continental states and stayed so busy, they rarely enjoyed the fruits of their labor. Sydney was planning a three-week trip to Paris for Doug's fortieth birthday, and she knew he would be over the moon excited. High on his bucket list was to see the Eiffel Tower, and she wanted to make that happen for him. Sydney wanted to take Ricky and Lucy with them and that took a bit of planning to make sure the dogs had the correct vaccinations and proper documentation, so they could travel abroad. To keep the dogs from having to ride below deck in a commercial plane, Syd hired a private jet to fly them to Paris. The thoughts of some ill fate happening to her pups made her cringe.

Once Sydney revealed her surprise to Doug and the trip grew closer, he could not stop talking about it. Every day, he researched places he wanted to visit, restaurants he wanted to try, and even browsed menus so that he would be prepared. He bought a book to learn to speak some French phrases as well as a translator app for his phone. They finished their projects and notified the clients that they would be taking a three-week sabbatical and provided the dates of their expected return as well as the next start up production date. Everything was all set, and they were packed and ready to fly.

Their plane landed during late night hours, and Doug expected to see a city covered in brilliant twinkling lights. Unfortunately, he only saw darkness and street lights. It could have been any city. The city labeled as the most romantic in the world was a little underwhelming in the beginning. Doug was expecting New York crossed with the Rocky Mountains crossed with the Canadian green lands. What he saw was not what he expected. They checked into the Hotel de Sers Champs Elysees, which was only a short distance from the Seine River and had been built in 1880. The magnificent Eiffel Tower and Arc de Triomphe could be seen from their suite above the golden triangle of France. The staff was quick to provide champagne and strawberries along with treats for the dogs. The hotel amenities were perfect, and they were welcomed with open arms. Doug was disappointed when the city streets were dirty, and the people of Paris appeared rude with few manners. It seemed that everyone smoked everywhere, and the Parisian residents would toss their cigarettes on the ground and stomp them out. Even Lucy and Ricky seemed down and out of sorts on their first walk. Instead of being excited and eager to explore, the pups held their noses up as though the air was offensive.

However, on the second night, the magic happened. Syd checked the pups into the hotel kennel, which provided baths and manicures, while she and Doug went out for the evening. The Eiffel

Tower stood 81 stories tall and sparkled with millions of glittering lights, which created a magical skyline. There were lovers snuggled on benches beneath massive overhanging tree limbs. No one was shy to show their passion, and it was contagious. Doug took Sydney in his arms several times as they strolled along the streets, and their passion that had dwindled a bit due to their overwhelming work schedules came alive again in the romantic atmosphere. Dinner at the Breizh Café was mouth-watering *delicieux*, and they ate flour crepes and galettes as their eyes rolled back in delight. Sydney licked whipped cream off Doug's fingers, and he could not wait for a midnight dessert in the hotel room.

The foggy streetscapes provided a mystical backdrop to watch the lights flickering atop the Tower. The street lamps glowed golden in the damp night and gave just enough darkness to create a seductive atmosphere. Doug spotted a tiny alleyway and pulled Sydney into it just enough to lean her against the brick wall and out of the street light. He grasped her hands and held them above her head, forbidding her to move away from him. With one hand he began unbuttoning her blouse and kissing her breasts releasing them from their camisole. Sydney rarely wore a bra, which created easy access to the softness of her nipples that immediately hardened beneath his hot tongue.

As he explored her breasts, she writhed beneath his weight, scratching her back on the brick but not feeling any pain because the pleasure was so intense. With his left hand he brought her hips up to him, and she wrapped her legs around his waist. When he loosened her wrists Sydney's hands wrapped around his head and guided him up to meet her mouth longing for his kiss. He pushed up and into her, and Syd could barely contain screams of delight that she feared would bring spectators or even police to the scene, but no one seemed to notice. Syd bit her lips in pleasure until she thought they would bleed as Doug pulled her toward him over and over again sending her ecstasy into an orbit that she hoped would never end.

Once they both came together and were out of breath, Syd eased her silk skirt back down onto her hips and straightened her clothes and hair as if nothing had just taken place that totally rocked her world. Her luxurious red cape had a hood, and she pulled it forward to cover he mess that Doug had made of her hair, so no one suspected they had just had great sex in that tiny, dark alley. Sydney wondered how many other couples had experienced the same pleasure in that same little, dark alley. They slipped back into the streets just as they had exited and giggled all the way back to their hotel suite. Sydney knew this was a night she would never forget.

As they returned to their room, Lucy and Ricky needed to go out so badly, they were jumping around the kennel with excitement. Doug offered to take them for a short walk while Syd took a shower to freshen up from their romp in the damp night. Both pups were ready to run and play when Syd returned from the shower, and they chased tennis balls as Doug bounced them off the walls. Once they tired and settled down between Sydney and Doug in their bed she relaxed looking up at the ceiling and could not believe they were actually in Paris. Doug's soft snores were steady, and she began to drift away into a deep sleep.

In the middle of the night, Sydney woke from a pain in her stomach, and she realized she was wet and shivering. She began heaving and ran to the bathroom to prevent vomiting in the bed. After several rounds of sickness, Doug knocked on the bathroom door to check on her.

"You alright, Babe? Can I get you something?" It worried Doug since he had only seen Sydney sick once during a bout with the flu. She was normally a picture of health.

"I'm fine. I must have eaten something that didn't settle well in my stomach. I'll be out in a few minutes. Go back to sleep, I'll be right in."

Sydney looked at herself in the mirror and was shocked at how pale her face appeared. She had dark circles under her eyes, and she looked scary. She didn't remember looking this way earlier in the evening. Great. Just what she needed. Food poisoning.

After drinking seltzer water, Syd crawled back into bed but was barely asleep when she became sick again. After a few episodes, she decided to take a blanket and pillow to lie in the bathroom floor. The tile was cool, and she was burning hot. When morning came and Doug saw her asleep on the floor, he was really worried. She looked dead lying in the floor, but when she heard him come in, she roused a bit.

"I think I need to see a doctor, Doug. I must have food poisoning. I can't stop vomiting, and I am very weak. Will you see if the hotel has a physician on call who could prescribe me a medication to ease my upset stomach?"

Doug called the front desk and within a half hour the doorbell rang to announce the staff physician.

"Bonjour, I am Dr. Phillipe; you have a sick Madame, no?" He came in and saw Sydney lying in the bed under thick covers. "What seems to be the trouble, Mademoiselle? How may I assist you?" His accent was very thick and was difficult to understand.

The older physician had beautiful white hair and a thick mustache that reminded her of the Wizard from Oz. He was tall, and his eyes had wrinkles at the edges as though he had laughed a lot during his lifetime as a doctor.

"I became sick last night after dinner, and I have vomited most of the night. I feel very weak and dizzy. My chest is also hurting, and my heart is beating very fast. I'm rarely ill, and this came on very quickly. I felt fine around 10:00 last night, but by midnight, I could barely walk. I think I may have food poisoning."

The old doc looked shocked, "Oh no, no Mademoiselle our food in Paris is par none. There is none better in the entire world. It would be dreadful if someone caught the poison from one of the fine restaurants in our city. It must be something else. Let me take some blood vials from you, and I can have tests run at our local facility.

We can see what it shows. Do you have heart history? Do you smoke? What did you do earlier in the evening?" He spoke quickly, and his French accent made it hard for Sydney to answer his questions as fast as he asked them. She wanted to make sure she understood everything he was asking her, so she could answer correctly.

"I am very healthy. I exercise daily, I eat healthy food, I do not smoke, and I run several miles each week. Yesterday, we went up the Eifel Tower but did not eat there. We strolled through the park and had dinner at the Breizhe Café, and it was delicious. I only had one glass of wine and then we walked through the city." She didn't share with him their little dark alley lovemaking tryst as she knew that could not have caused her sickness.

Dr. Philippe drew three tubes of blood, scribbled orders for the lab, and told her he would call her as soon as the test results were complete. He gave her some medicine for nausea and instructed her to lie around for the day and take it easy. That was the easy part, as Syd's legs would barely hold her long enough to walk from one room to another. After he left, she drifted into a deep sleep and hoped the worst had passed. Right before dark, the phone rang, and Dr. Philippe was calling to report her test results.

"Madame, you should come to the facility please. We need to run a few more tests and take a closer look at your heart. You may have suffered a mild heart attack, but we must do more testing to make certain. I would feel much better if we could keep you overnight for monitoring."

Sydney felt numb all over and turned pale as she listened to his possible diagnosis.

"What is it Syd? You look like you've seen a ghost. Are you okay? Is he phoning in some antibiotics? Syd? Sydney? For God's sake, say something." Doug was beginning to panic as she just stared ahead. Finally, she turned and said:

"Dr. Philippe thinks I may have had a mild heart attack. He wants me to come to the hospital and stay tonight for more tests.

A heart attack? I'm too young for a heart attack. That's just crazy. I don't have cardiac problems, no one in my family does that I'm aware of. That is just absurd."

Sydney sat on the side of bed as she hung up the phone.

"Pack a bag, and let's go get this checked out. We can't take a chance on something like this being accurate. I'm sure it is just a mistake, but we need to make certain."

As Doug called the front desk to arrange the kennel for Ricky and Lucy, Sydney stammered in a daze at the thought she might have had a heart attack. This had to be a mistake, it was just craziness.

Once they arrived at the hospital, Sydney was registered and admitted. The nurse gave her a blue gown just like the ones in the States with the backside open and covering very little. A lab technician came in and started an IV with what looked like plain tap water running through it.

"This is just for hydration since you lost so much fluid vomiting. I will be in shortly to add medication to your IV bag. Just lie back, and take it easy. A few more nurses will come in asking you quite a few questions. I apologize, as some of them may be redundant, but the answers go to different departments in the facility and are needed to hopefully find a proper diagnosis for you so that we can treat it quickly. How are you feeling now? Any nausea? Pain?"

Sydney shook her head realizing she had not eaten anything since earlier in the day, and she should be hungry, but she wasn't. She drifted off to sleep and was awakened by someone violently vomiting and realized it was her. Doug was standing beside her with a basin in his hand and holding her hair back. She was looking ashen and worse than earlier in the morning and he was really worried about her.

After 24 hours, Sydney had been pricked by every hospital staff member for every test they needed and still no conclusion. Some of her lab values were high, some were low. She was dehydrated, anemic, and had no appetite. A team of physicians were called in for consultation, but she was barely alert. They all agreed she was too thin and needed protein to retain the muscle mass she was beginning to lose, but every time she even smelled food, she began gagging. Her hair was dull, and her cute little curves were leaving. An ultrasound was ordered to look for masses or suspicious polyps but first more blood tests were performed. Sydney just wanted to go home, to her home and to her bed.

Ricky and Lucy were exploding with energy when Doug went by the kennel to check on them. They didn't understand why they were being kept in cages while their parents were absent. Doug knew how badly Sydney was feeling because she had not even asked about her beloved pups. The doctors decided to allow Syd to go back to her hotel on bedrest while all of her tests were processed because her condition was unchanged, and they had no conclusive reason to keep her there.

Once back at the hotel, she was carried upstairs to their suite on a stretcher because she had no strength, and Doug thought she looked like she was surely dying. He checked the dogs out of the kennel, hoping they would perk up Sydney's spirits. They bounded into the hotel room, licked her face, and snuggled underneath the covers behind Syd's knees. She didn't stir or even attempt to pet them.

Four days passed with no improvement, and Doug cancelled their flight home. Every test came back with an inconclusive result. No answers were forthcoming, and she looked wretched. Doug called Matthew Daniels to let him know about Sydney's sickness. Doug brought him up to speed in case he needed to answer any questions that might come up regarding any of the projects they were working on together but asked Matt not to disturb her if possible because she needed every bit of sleep she could get. He didn't mention to Matthew that he truly thought she was dying, and they didn't even know why. The French doctors on her team showed very little concern, and Doug requested that additional specialists be called.

Another week went by, and Sydney began to make a little improvement in walking and balance. Her tiny legs were so weak from bedrest that they began to shake each time she tried to walk across the room. On day 21 of the trip Syd and Doug, along with Lucy and Ricky, flew back to Tennessee with hopes that healing would come faster once home. Sydney couldn't work or focus, and her short-term memory had really become an issue. Her body was experiencing general soreness, and no food agreed with her digestive system. She tried to talk to Doug but called him everyone's name but his own. It was as though she had dementia, but she was surely too young, and the onset was too sudden. During the nights, she would call out her dad's name as though she could see him. That truly frightened Doug. The doctors had ruled out meningitis, a bacterial infection, mononucleosis or sepsis. They found several diagnoses that were not the answer, but none that led to the correct one.

One night, Sydney was lying in bed and she felt a strange stirring in her belly that made her jump. With no medical education or personal experience, Sydney knew immediately what was the answer they had been waiting for this entire time. She was feeling life inside her. Afraid to move, she lay very still on her back and knew she had to see an OB physician the next day.

— CHAPTER 21 —

As Sydney sat in the waiting room, she glanced around and saw women of all ages. Some were young and pregnant; others were older and apparently seeing Dr. Jacobs for other symptoms. After a simple blood test, the doctor confirmed that Sydney was indeed pregnant and explained that she had just experienced an intense episode of first trimester sickness.

The OB nurse reassured Sydney, "Not every woman experiences only morning sickness; some are sick in the evenings, and in some more severe cases are sick all day long. The ills of pregnancy are as individual as the woman herself. No two are alike."

"How can this be? Every test known to mankind has been run on me and none of them came up with a positive pregnancy test."

"Did they run a pregnancy test?" Dr. Jacobs wanted to know.

"Surely, they did," Syd said with no assurance whatsoever. She explained the events in Paris and how worried they were regarding the lack of a diagnosis found. There had been no symptoms of pregnancy; she was having her cycle each month, she was not experiencing morning sickness in the sense that she imagined a pregnancy would bring, and she wasn't moody or crying a lot. Her breasts had been tender, but she thought that was because of lifting some pretty heavy engine parts with Doug prior to their trip. Sydney sat in the lab anxiously awaiting more results when the nurse called her name, and she felt her legs shaking as she tried to compose herself.

"Are you okay, Ms. James? You look a little nervous," the nurse's observation made her feel no comfort at all. "The doctor will be in to see you in just a few minutes. Go ahead and remove your clothes and put on this gown, tying it in the back. He will want to perform an exam, and I will be right here with you."

Sydney began to feel as though she would vomit again when suddenly everything went black. She woke up on a stretcher with a pillow under her head and a sheet covering her body. As Dr. Jacobs came into the room, he looked concerned, which alarmed Sydney. He explained that her body was trying to reject the pregnancy.

"What does that mean?" asked Syd, completely confused. "I have never heard of that. Am I having a miscarriage? I have not missed a cycle, but I am not bleeding at the moment."

"No, it is a different phenomenon where your brain is signaling your body that it is not hosting a fetus, but your natural body signals are not agreeing. It will level out, but every woman's body is different, and while some stabilize quickly, some are not in harmony for the entire 40 weeks. You are in good shape, and you are 20 weeks pregnant according to your HCG level. This means no matter how your body reacts, you only have 20 weeks to endure and hopefully enjoy some of your pregnancy. Your body is confused as to what your brain wants during this time. Your systems aren't sure whether to mimic a heart attack, a panic attack, or a stomach virus. Once you balance out, you will feel more normal again. But remember pregnancy is not a normal state for a woman, so your body will react differently for the next 18 to 20 weeks. It is a wonderful miracle to experience, and I hope that you can stay well enough to enjoy your last few months."

Sydney lay staring at the ceiling trying to absorb everything Dr. Jacobs had told her. For a while, she completely forgot about Doug. Oh God Doug...what would he say? They hadn't made love as much lately because she had been sick for so many weeks, and he didn't even suggest it when he saw that she felt tired. He had begun to think she was seriously ill with cancer or a chronic disease of some sort that would rack her body with pain or disabilities that would rob her life of its joy.

Syd slowly sat up, and she felt a little better. She took a sip of water that Dr. Jacobs gave her, and after he left the room, she was able to redress to be dismissed by his nurse. Sydney made a follow up appointment for the first ultrasound, so that she and Doug could hear the baby's heartbeat for the first time together. The nurse gave Sydney a bag of prenatal vitamins, some pamphlets for her to read, and websites for her to research the unusual symptoms she was experiencing. She was placed on a limited cardiac diet that would minimize her symptoms and give her energy from the extra protein. She was ordered to stay on bed rest at home as long as she was not vomiting, but if she could not keep her meals down, she would have to be hospitalized for nutrition for herself and the baby.

Baby...B-A-B-Y, a word Syd had never connected with herself. Already, this little thing inside her was controlling her life; it was dictating her work schedule and even her thoughts were consumed with this little peanut sized being floating around in her belly. Suddenly, Sydney was not sure she wanted this to be her life. She had worked so hard for so many years to be successful and build her company. She travelled frequently, nationally and abroad, and how could she take care of a baby with her schedule? She had two dogs that she adored, and they were enough for her. She had never wanted to be tied down with children or even a husband, and she and Doug worked well because their schedules were the same. A family had never figured into her short- or long-term goals.

The nurse started to leave after giving Sydney instructions and samples when Sydney stopped her.

"Could I ask you a question?" Sydney was embarrassed but had to know the answer.

"Of course, anything," replied the nurse as she came back over to Sydney's chair.

"What, what if I didn't want to keep the baby?"

Sydney waited for her answer afraid to breathe.

"You mean give it up for adoption? There are many couples who would love to adopt your baby. The wait list for an infant is two years or more, and we could give you contact information for agencies or attorneys who handle legal adoptions."

"No, I don't mean adoption. What about an abortion? What if I don't want to carry the baby? I don't think I can do this. My life is not ideal for a child. I have no family, I have no one, and I have an all-consuming career. I just don't think I want to carry this pregnancy out." Sydney didn't even realize that tears were pouring down her cheeks as she tried to explain her circumstances to the nurse.

"I'm sorry, but you are too far along for an abortion. You are five months pregnant, and your baby already weighs about three pounds. The heart, lungs, and endocrine system is fully developed. At your next visit, you will see the baby and hear the heartbeat on the ultrasound. and we can tell you the sex of your baby. We can perform a 4-D ultrasound, and you can see its tiny mouth, lips, and face and even if there is hair on his or her little head. Your baby can suck its thumb, smile, and stick its tongue out. I know you said you have no family, but if I may ask, what about the father? Will he want to be involved in the life of the baby? That would be my first suggestion for a support system if you have an ongoing relationship. Have you ever thought of a future with children? At your age, Sydney, a first pregnancy may be your last, so let's get you excited about this baby that is on the way! Make an appointment for next Tuesday, and if you would like to bring him to see the ultrasound with you, please do. It is usually a very happy and emotional visit. You will get the first photos of your little one, and you will most likely feel much different in a week's time. Go home and get some rest, and if you do not feel any better in a few days, give us a call and we can admit you for IV nutritional infusion. Start taking your prenatal vitamins immediately, and the Zofran will help with the nausea and vomiting. If you will take your chart out to the front desk, they will schedule your appointment for you and file the insurance papers."

Sydney could hardly focus as she drove back to the garage. She ran a red light and almost hit an oncoming car, swerving just in time to miss it. She walked into the garage to find Doug in his office, focused on a screen, and he didn't see her come in. She tapped on his door, and he jumped when he saw her, but then his eyes lit up with a smile stretching across his face. He was always so happy to see her. He thought she had been upstairs working all morning and had not interrupted her. Doug knew immediately that something was wrong by the look in her eyes. He could see that she had been crying and was holding a bag of medicine.

"Syd, what's wrong? Where have you been? I thought you were upstairs working. Have you seen a doctor? Why didn't you let me know you were going out, I would have gone with you."

At the sight of him, she broke into tears and flopped down on the couch in his office. She wept uncontrollably until he calmed her by stroking her hair as he held her close. Finally, Sydney stopped sobbing and looked up into his sky-blue eyes that were the windows to the man that adored her.

"This is very hard to explain, but I will try to make it short and clear for you. I don't understand everything Dr. Jacobs told me, but apparently my body has been fighting against itself and trying to win a war inside me. All of the tests they ran in Paris and since have not led to a diagnosis. My body has not reacted the way a woman's body normally would but it seems...get ready for this...it seems that the simple but also complex diagnosis is that I am pregnant. Twenty weeks pregnant Doug! My cycle has continued, and the vomiting and weakness is due to the fact that I have a human growing inside me. None of the tests in Paris revealed it because my body has some strange phenomenon that doesn't want to be pregnant, so I have not experienced normal symptoms of pregnancy like simple morning sickness, breast tenderness, and mood swings. I have instead displayed symptoms of a heart attack, a gall bladder attack, and even some types of cancers. The tests have all produced what they call a psychosis because they are fake, pure, and simple. My body is trying to reject the real diagnosis....a baby. When Dr. Jacobs ran the HCG level, it came back five months pregnant."

Her eyes were overflowing with the biggest tears Doug had ever seen, and he sat silent and stunned. It took him a minute to realize that she was staring at him waiting for a reaction.

"Why aren't you saying anything? I asked for an abortion, but I'm too far along. The nurse told me I could give it up for adoption because there is a long waiting list for infant babies in America. I may be this sick the entire pregnancy, and my work may have to be put on hold. I may even have to be admitted for prenatal failure to thrive if I can't keep food down or the baby could die before I even give birth. What am I going to do, Doug? How on Earth can I have a child? I don't have time. I don't have room in my life, and I don't even have room in my loft. This is the worst thing in the world! Say something dammit. "

As Doug took both of Syd's hands in his, a smile came across his face that could not hide his excitement.

"Is it the worst thing, Syd? A baby? A family? Our baby, our family. What could be better? This isn't the worst thing it is the best thing ever. You can't give it up for adoption. I would die of a broken heart. I cannot believe we're having a baby."

Doug jumped up and pulled her up by her wrists. He lifted her shirt and starting kissing her belly, which was barely rounded with their baby inside. He was crying and laughing at the same time kissing all over her stomach. He unbuttoned her shirt and kissed her breasts that were now fuller and driving him crazy. He told her over and over how much he loved her and their new baby boy or girl, and he wanted both of them so much. He slowly began to undress her, and for the first time in weeks, Sydney's sex drive returned. As they made love in his office, he held her tighter than ever and was so gentle and tender with her.

Doug looked at her with love in his eyes.

"I thought you were dying and that I was losing you. Sydney, I have never loved you more. I know everything will be fine with your health. I am so happy, I can't even tell you how much. We can buy a bigger place to live with a big yard for Lucy and Ricky and a nursery for the baby. Or we can blow out a wall upstairs and make a huge nursery and add a bathroom. Hell, half of the upstairs warehouse is attic space right next to our bedroom. We could turn that into a terrific nursery and bath for the baby."

In his mind Doug had it all figured out, and he was ecstatic. Sydney was still wasn't thrilled and not sure if this was the life she really wanted.

— CHAPTER 22 —

Doug couldn't wait until the next Tuesday and sang all week while he worked diligently on PDOB35 that was to be tested in Washington before the Summit Committee to approve a safety mechanism for garage doors. He tried to focus, but his mind drifted to the baby and Sydney. He was worried about her health, as she still had not bounced back to her normal activity. She was holding down more food, but she was somber and withdrawn. He was excited to see their baby on the ultrasound, but Syd didn't really want to talk about it. She was still absorbing it all while Doug was having plans drawn to remodel the second floor and create a massive nursery suite fit for a little prince or princess. His entire life, Doug dreamed of being a father. He had loved his dad so much and respected the life he had lived and the legend he left. His mother would be over the moon when he told her but was anxiously waiting until Sydney gave him the green light to make the announcement. Doug had bought Sydney a beautiful three-carat, emerald cut engagement ring and had planned to propose to her in Paris, but when she became ill and was hospitalized, he decided to put it on hold. Now the baby was foremost in their thoughts and would stall his proposal for a while, but Doug was willing to wait. He was actually going to have the family that he had dreamed of for as long as he remembered, and this baby could not come fast enough.

Tuesday finally arrived, and Sydney was glowing. She looked beautiful with her tiny mound barely visible in her beautiful cashmere tunic, leggings, and knee-high boots. She was beginning to finally gain a little weight, and Doug was so thankful that the vomiting had almost subsided. Her color was once again pink, and the circles under her eyes were not as obvious. He still heard her vomiting at night but not as often and he was thankful. Dr. Jacobs' office was full of pregnant women and their partners to support them. There were young women, older women, some were mixed couples, some were same sex couples, but all were happy and excited about their coming arrivals. Doug hoped that Sydney took note of all the types of families in the room, so that she would know theirs would be a perfect family as long as they had each other.

The nurse called Sydney's name, and it was their turn to visit with the doctor. He asked Sydney a lot of questions after shaking Doug's hand and congratulating him. Dr. Jacobs said he would be following her pregnancy and delivering the baby. He was very thorough in his questions and seemed concerned about Syd's health as well as the baby's. After a few minutes of examining her, he slid his stool over to Syd as she lay on the stretcher. He addressed both of them and told them he wanted to discuss something very important that he recommended.

"Sydney, due to your age and this being your first pregnancy, the chance of delivering a baby with Downs Syndrome is higher than average. I suggest we perform a test called amniocentesis, where the fetus is tested for this disability. The probability increases in mothers who are over 30 giving birth for the first time. Due to your severe illness in the first and into the second trimester, I'd like to perform this with a needle biopsy on Thursday. It is not painful but it is very important to determine if the baby is healthy."

He was very detailed in his description of the procedure and assured them this was necessary.

"What happens if it is positive and shows that our baby has Downs Syndrome? Is the baby aborted? Will it make a difference in the birth or care after the birth?" Sydney became distressed the more he told them.

"There is no change in the pre- or postpartum care. However, it is good to know, so that you can educate yourself and research the extensive care for your baby, expectations, and extended care as your child grows. Children with Downs are extremely loving and lead wonderful lives, but require more than normal time, dedication, and patience, and their life expectancy is not as long."

Sydney lay back on the stretcher while the ultrasonographer put clear jelly on her stomach and ran a wand across it. The monitor sprang to life, and a squishing heart beat sounded loudly. As the tech brought the wand across her stomach, a grainy little face appeared to be looking right at them as to say hello. The heartbeat was fast as they heard the *swish-swish, swish-swish, swish-swish* of the tiny muscle.

"The heartbeat is 169 beats per minute," the tech explained.

"Is that bad?" asked Sydney while Doug just stared at the little face, mesmerized.

"No, not bad. Just some say that girls have a faster heart rate," as she smiled.

"It's a girl?" asked Doug.

"Well, I'm not sure, let's get him or her to turn and see if we can see the sex of the baby. As she pointed the mouse and clicked several times creating red lines from X to X on the screen, she explained she was measuring the baby's bones. She began massaging Sydney's stomach and gently pushing trying to turn the baby, so that the tiny genitals would be exposed. The little thing was sucking a thumb and moving arms and legs.

"Ten little fingers and 10 little toes," she told them as she pointed to each one. "There is the little nose, lips, and look at all that hair." All that Doug could see was the shape of the face, but he couldn't really make out any hair on the head. "Oh my goodness, it looks like you have yourself a little princess! Get ready for lots of pink, Daddy."

Tears were rolling down Doug's cheeks, and he knew she would wrap him around her little finger just like her mommy had years before. He and Sydney were holding hands, both crying, and Sydney knew at that moment that her baby would be loved regardless of gender, health, or any other complications that would arise. She finally realized that they were a family, and she already adored this little angel. The tech printed off four pictures that were detailed and listed "James" as the baby's last name and "Girl" as her gender. Both mommy and daddy were thrilled.

After the doctor's appointment, Sydney and Doug went to a local deli for lunch and began discussing everything they just experienced at the doctor visit. There was so much information thrown at them, and their heads were confused and swimming with all of the decisions to be made. Syd was still concerned about the upcoming amniocentesis, but she knew that no matter the results, she would love their baby girl and provide the best treatment available if needed.

"What would you like to name her?" Doug asked.

Sydney thought for a moment and said, "I'm not sure but I'd like her to have your last name."

Doug considered this and then suggested that they name her O'Brian-James to include both their last names.

"We still have a few months to decide, but we better get busy building a nursery for her."

They wandered into the mall and went straight to a baby store where Doug bought the biggest stuffed animal they had. Looking at the tiny shoes and dresses created an excitement in Sydney that she had never experienced. She was going to be a mommy. It was such a foreign feeling but was growing stronger every time the baby kicked. Sidney wished her parents were here for this special time in her life. They would have been amazing grandparents.

— CHAPTER 23 —

The next week contractors crashed through the brick wall in their master bedroom and exposed a huge space that would soon be the baby's nursery, play room and include a bath. During the renovation, Doug and Syd moved their personal things into the apartment by the river walk and worked during the day either in their office there or in Doug's office in the garage. The amniocentesis results came back negative and they were so relieved to be able to move forward and know their little peanut was healthy. As Sydney's belly grew bigger, she found it more difficult to get around the engine room and help Doug lift any heavy products. They had decided to name the baby Claire O'Brian James after Sydney's mother and Doug's last name as well as hers. The vomiting had subsided, and Sydney actually felt better than she had in weeks. Her skin was rosy, and her hair was long, thick, and shiny.

The nursery project was coming along beautifully, and Syd decided on pale baby pink and gray paint. The room was massive and would be perfect as she grew and needed larger furniture. For the moment, it was furnished with a brass Cinderella carriage baby bed, antique dresser, chest, and changing table. The bed skirt had layers of pink and gray ruffles and enormous bows eat each corner, creating the look of clouds for their baby. Sydney had found an antique chandelier with tiny crystals for the vaulted ceiling that sparkled in the morning sunlight which streamed through the floor to ceiling windows on two sides of the room. Doug had painted an old rocker they discovered in a resale store, and Syd bought thick pillows to support her back so she could rock the baby to sleep. The dark hardwood floors were shiny underneath a furry pink shag rug that would keep her tiny feet nice and toasty as she learned to walk. Sydney had ordered baby elephant prints and stuffed animals with big bows on their ears. Her closet was already full of beautiful baby clothing, and there was nothing she would need for months. Matt Daniels had sent a baby travel set that included a car seat, stroller, and all of the expensive necessities that apparently parents could not live without when the baby came. They were registered at Baby's R Us, FAO Schwarz, and Target for any items they thought would be needed, but Sydney was nervous if there were still important items they may have forgotten—like diapers, tiny nail clippers, or one of those bulb nose squeezers. How could such a tiny human need so much to survive? Lucy and Ricky knew something was up and spent hours sniffing the new baby area where attic space once had been. Lucy didn't mind when Sydney's stomach came alive with kicks and movement, but Ricky, on the other hand, growled each time the baby moved. Syd hoped they would learn to love baby Claire when she came home.

A week prior to her due date, Sydney's blood pressure escalated, and her feet and hands began to swell. Sydney started seeing little black spots in her eyes, and Dr. Jacobs admitted her into the hospital for pre-eclampsia. He explained to Doug that there was a chance that Sydney would need a cesarean section for her safety as well as baby Claire when the contractions began. Syd was adamant about finishing out her pregnancy at home tying up loose ends in the nursery and her work at SCJ, but Dr. Jacobs refused to listen. He was strict with the admission orders, so Sydney went along with him. Doug worked night and day completing their last project and intended to take the next few weeks off to enjoy the time with the baby and Sydney.

At 4:00 in the morning, Sydney woke up to find that her bed was wet. She called for the nurse and told her that she was hurting in her back and thought that her water may have broken. The contractions started, and Sydney had never felt such pain. Doug had been by her side since she was admitted and would not go home except to shower, change clothes, and care for the dogs. He sat by her side and fed her ice chips while her contractions continued to come faster. Doug's mother and sister sat in the family room, anxiously waiting for the baby to arrive. Two hours turned into four hours, then six hours later, and still no baby. Sydney had been given an epidural to ease the pain, but it was beginning to wear off and the pain was back again. After eight hours, Dr. Jacobs came in and told them he was preparing the OR team for a C-section. Sydney was beginning to tire, and the baby's heart rate was dropping. Dr. Jacobs wanted to avoid fetal distress and was afraid Sydney would not be able to push if they waited much longer. Doug was led to a room to scrub and change into a surgical gown, cap, and gloves. His stomach was turning flips, and he thought he might vomit.

"No matter what you do, Doug, don't faint," instructed Dr. Jacobs. "If you faint, we will leave you in the floor as we tend to your baby and her mother. We will have to let you lie there, and hopefully, you'll recover, but our first priority is to take care of baby and mommy."

He laughed at Doug and knew this was a scary procedure for both moms and dads, but especially dads.

After wheeling Sydney to the operating room and gathering his staff and equipment Dr. Jacobs was scrubbed and sterile, "Here we go... Everyone ready?"

As they played soft music, each staff member worked with precise steps. They knew exactly what to do and reassured Sydney through the entire birthing process. Doug sat at her head and could not see the cuts they made on her stomach to bring the baby out, but he could hear the doctor give orders and ask his team for specific instruments. In what seemed like only seconds, he heard a tiny squeal, then a louder wail as Dr. Jacobs brought up a greasy little thing with wet curly hair and swollen eyes, and she began screaming as he held her upside down by her ankles.

"Daddy, Mommy, you have a perfect little girl," Dr. Jacobs announced, and as he held her wet head, her big eyes looked around the room as to announce her important arrival. Dr. Jacobs laughed under his mask, always in awe of the miracle of birth. The nurses took her and began vigorously massaging her little legs and arms, placing eye drops in her eyes, and a warming cap on her head. The team began stitching Sydney's stomach, and when they were finished, they lay the baby on her chest and instructed Doug to bring his face close to mommy and baby, so they could bond. Tiny little fingers and toes started wiggling while her arms were flailing about. Her big blue eyes looked at them as to say, "Hello, I'm happy to finally meet you both." Doug and Sydney were crying as they marveled at the miracle lying between them.

Sydney was taken to a nursing room for the night, and the next morning she would be allowed to receive visitors. After sleeping deeply through the night, Sydney woke when the hospital door opened, and Doug walked in hiding behind a beautiful vase with an enormous bouquet of three dozen pink roses. The nurse had brought Claire to Sydney for nursing, and she was wearing a tiny pink bow in her hair. Doug could not wait to hold his perfect new daughter and kiss her mother. Rosy chubby cheeks and long skinny legs made her tiny six-pound body look a little like a spider, and to Doug she was the most beautiful baby in the world. Her bright blue eyes looked like his and the strawberry blond mat on her head was a combination of both Syd and Doug's hair colors. She looked up at her daddy as if she knew him immediately and was there to wrap him around her tiny finger. As she yawned, her pink gums looked like a little granny laughing without dentures.

Doug placed the roses on the bedside table and kissed Sydney firmly on her mouth. He was careful not to hug too tightly because he knew she would be in pain from the C-section.

"Thank you for all your hard work. You really took one for the team bringing this sweet princess into our lives. I thought life couldn't get any better and yet I have a feeling it's only the beginning of great memories to be made." Doug had tears rolling down his face, and Sydney looked up at him holding their daughter. Her heart felt like it would burst with pride. He handed Claire back to her mother and said he had one more gift he had left in the hallway. He brought in a pink fuzzy elephant much bigger than Claire was in his arms, and he sat it on the bed with both of his girls. On the elephant's arm was a black velvet box, and for a moment, Syd didn't notice it.

"This is Ellie the Elephant, and she has something she needs to ask you."

Doug had a crooked grin on his lips.

When Sydney took a second look at the stuffed animal, she saw the box snuggled into the arm. Sydney looked at Doug with a questioning look in her eyes. Doug took the box from the rubber band on the elephant's wrist and opened it for Sydney to see.

"You are the love of my life Sydney and now you have given me the best gift I could ever receive. I want to spend my life making you happy and becoming the man that you believe me to be. I will love you until my heart stops, and there is no more breath in my body. I didn't know love until I met you, and I now have more love in my life than I deserve. I cannot imagine my life without you or Claire. Will you spend your life with me Syd? Will you marry me?"

As Sydney looked at the magnificent diamond engagement ring in the box, she knew that her life now had more meaning than she had ever thought possible, all because of this man standing before her. She had been emotionally closed off for many years, and yet Doug saw through her and gave her the time and space to break through her steel heart. She was no longer afraid of hurt or rejection. She now completely understood the depth of love he had for her reflected in his beautiful blue eyes. She looked at Doug and then down at the same eyes staring back at her from her daughter's sweet face.

"I love you, Doug, and yes, I would love to marry you." And without waiting a second he slipped the ring on her left hand.

As Doug kissed Sidney he whispered, "I love you more than you will ever know, and I don't ever want to live a day without you and Claire, and of course, Ricky and Lucy."

Tears were streaming down their cheeks as they looked down at the sweet sleeping baby in her arms and knew they were ready for this new life of love, happiness, and hope for the future.